UNLOCKED
AN ANTHOLOGY

ANA BRAZIL   EDIE CAY   MARI ANNE CHRISTIE
ANNE M. BEGGS   REBECCA D'HARLINGUE
LINDA ULLESEIT   C.V. LEE   KATHRYN PRITCHETT

EDITED BY
MARI ANNE CHRISTIE AND EDIE CAY

COVER DESIGN BY
MARI ANNE CHRISTIE

Copyright © 2022 by Paper Lantern Writers

All rights reserved.

No part of this book may be reproduced in any form or by any electronic or mechanical means, including information storage and retrieval systems, without written permission from the author, except for the use of brief quotations in a book review.

Dedicated to the members of **SHINE with Paper Lantern Writers**, *whose support and encouragement make our writing lives that much more fulfilling. The world of historical fiction is large, and we are delighted to share our little corner with you.*

WHO KNOWS WHAT TREASURES WILL BE FOUND WHEN THIS ANCIENT TRUNK IS FINALLY UNLOCKED?

The Happy Heart: A groovy, tarot-soaked tale about a late-blooming flower child seeking enlightenment.
Trust No One: In World War II Washington, D.C., a baby shower is overshadowed by espionage, ambition, and betrayal.
True Legacy: A 1920's inheritance chronicles secrets told and secrets kept, shaping a family's story.
Threadbare Linens: During the American Civil War, a family is torn apart by filicide and assorted family warfare.
A Rarefied Gift: A Regency London mystery about adult twins searching for answers surrounding their birth.
The Shell: In 1679 Amsterdam, a wife struggles to forget a past love.
Joanna's Choice: A Renaissance story of a woman who longs to escape her scandalous past.
The Dragon Lord: A Medieval tale of romance and religion vying for supremacy at the Winter Solstice.

CONTENTS

The Happy Heart *By Kathryn Pritchett*	1
Trust No One *By Ana Brazil*	17
True Legacy *By Linda Ulleseit*	41
Threadbare Linens *By Mari Anne Christie*	65
A Rarefied Gift *By Edie Cay*	87
The Shell *By Rebecca D'Harlingue*	119
Joanna's Choice *By C.V. Lee*	129
The Dragon Lord - A Winter Solstice Tale *By Anne M. Beggs*	167
About Paper Lantern Writers	205
Authors' Note	207

THE HAPPY HEART
BY KATHRYN PRITCHETT

BERKELEY, CALIFORNIA, SUMMER OF 1972

Celeste hummed along to the Zombies as she hunted for her best client's favorite tarot deck. "What's your name, who's your daddy? Is he rich, is he rich like me?" She rifled through the battered wooden chest with the heart-shaped lock where she kept her card decks, casting aside the jewel-toned Rider-Waite and the black-and-white Hermetic. At last, her fingers grasped the mauve velvet pouch that held the Aquarian deck with all those dreamy knights. She removed the pouch from the chest that sat in the window beneath the rainbow-hued title of her shop, The Happy Heart.

She'd found the chest at Jack's Antiques on Ashby, not long after she arrived in Berkeley. Amidst the old-timey glass medicine bottles and tarnished silver pieces, it had seemed like a hopeful—and useful—addition to her ground-floor apartment off Telegraph Avenue.

In the five years since she'd hung out her psychic shingle,

Celeste had used it to store various relics that had survived her move north, including her mother's well-worn runes and a cracked crystal ball. To accommodate the latter she'd needed to remove a broken panel that had once provided a false bottom to the chest. No more secrets would be hidden there.

At the dawning of the Age of Aquarius, she'd hoped to enter a respectable profession, like bookkeeping, while working on her macrame art at night. But when the only clerical work she found proved tedious—turned out she didn't actually want to file papers all day for a plumbing company—she'd channeled her mother in hopes of making a living from the dead.

Sadly, she wasn't anything like the queenly mystic her mother embodied in her shop off Sunset. There, her mother's aquiline profile and haughty deportment had been sharp as a sword; she ruled in the element of Air. Whereas Celeste—née Gladys—was made of blowsier material, like sunflowers gone to seed at summer's end. With her frizzy copper curls and short, dumpy body, she was firmly grounded in Earth, often in the mud.

"Play to your strengths, darling," her mother had always said. Thus, Celeste's short-lived dip in the clerical pool. But when she'd left that job, and it looked like she'd have no other option but to camp out in People's Park with the rest of the much-younger flower children, she decided to take a crack at the family business. She took on a new name that was both mystical and practical. Instead of something vaguely ethnic like Zara or tie-dyed like Starchild, Gladys settled on Celeste. As for the shop, she chose a name that was sure to attract clients.

"People come to me because I deal in happiness," her mother would often say, before she'd decided to follow her latest beau to a commune in Chiapas. Then she'd explain that what most clients wanted was advice about love or money.

Preferably both. "So, I give them what they want. If they leave a little happier, they'll return for another shot of happiness."

Celeste decided to advertise happiness up front. But what to name her shop that would do just that? Finding the chest with the carved heart seemed like a sign, and The Happy Heart was born.

Mrs. X's heart was none too happy, which kept her crossing the Bay Bridge to visit Celeste. Oh, she had half of the happiness equation—a fancy house in Pacific Heights, a beautiful German stallion named Fritz and all the Pucci frocks a society matron could desire. But the other half—love—was sorely missing.

Mr. X had made a fortune in oil, which allowed him to live by the San Francisco Bay rather than a brackish pond in Texas or a forsaken lake in Missouri. That's where he'd first met Mrs. X and added her to his collection, though she wasn't the last or showiest of his acquisitions.

Today, she slipped into the shop wearing a silk scarf in a wavy turquoise-and-lime pattern over her raven locks. The sea-kissed scarf gave Mrs. X the appearance of a mythical mermaid, washed ashore on the streets of Berkeley in the summer of 1972. Though its subtle sheen would be more fitting on a yacht in Cannes than in this small storefront draped with paisley fabric acquired from street vendors who took a reading now and then as payment.

Celeste stood near the little side table where she'd lit the incense Mrs. X preferred—a heady mix of patchouli and musk. She greeted her with a hug before grabbing the feline Luna from the scrolled Victorian armchair she'd also found at Jack's.

THE HAPPY HEART

She gestured for Mrs. X to take a seat, grateful that Luna's silvery hair wouldn't be so noticeable on her client's white gaucho pants.

"Celeste, I don't know what I would have done if you couldn't see me today," said Mrs. X, removing her dark, double-bridged sunglasses to reveal red-rimmed eyes.

"But, of course," said Celeste in a cooing fashion she hoped would put Mrs. X in a receptive state of mind. She would need to work hard to impart happiness today.

"I'm at my wit's end. He's really done it now, shown up in Herb Cain's column with that little hussy on his arm. Honestly, he revels in my humiliation."

"Men can be such idiots," said Celeste, already shuffling the cards in a practiced manner. She set the deck face down on the maroon velvet cloth she'd snagged from a Goodwill bin, then asked Mrs. X to divide them into three piles and combine them in whatever order she felt appropriate. Celeste pulled ten cards from the top and laid them out in a traditional Celtic Cross.

She turned over the first card.

"The Queen of Pentacles. Well now, that's certainly you, my dear. No matter what your husband does or with whom, you will always be his queen with many resources at your disposal."

So far, so good.

Next came the obstacle card, the thing that was blocking Mrs. X's happiness. Celeste slowly turned over the card.

They both stared silently at the tall wooden tower with flames leaping out of the turreted top, surrounded by lightning bolts.

"I'm done for," said Mrs. X.

"Now remember, this is not just an obstacle, but also an

opportunity," said Celeste in a low murmur, appropriate for talking a jumper off the Golden Gate Bridge.

She quickly turned the card directly above, which showed an idyllic castle seen through a rose-covered bower. "This is the root of the problem—your desire for a castle on a hill, a place of security and love."

Mrs. X nodded as she fished around for a Kleenex in her fringed suede bag. "Is that so wrong? It's all I've ever wanted."

"No, but that desire has kept you locked in an unrealistic vision," said Celeste, turning over the image of a blindfolded woman bearing crossed swords. "Time to take action."

She flipped the fifth card to reveal a man and a woman holding cups and staring deeply into each other's eyes.

"Perhaps there's someone else in my future?" said Mrs. X with a lilt of desperation in her voice.

Celeste paused for a moment. That was one interpretation, one that would empower Mrs. X to leave her husband. But too much happiness was not in Celeste's best interest. She countered quickly. "Or... there's a reconciliation ahead." She flipped the next card and nearly swore when she saw a cloaked figure walking away from a bevy of cups.

"Sure looks like I'm supposed to leave my past behind." Mrs. X's brow crumpled as she looked up.

Celeste took a deep breath and prayed the King of Pentacles would appear in the self-perception position. She could work with that, tell Mrs. X that Mr. X was meant to be part of her life, that the Tower card's prominent placement just meant she needed to renew her efforts to win him back. No doubt that would ensure her ongoing patronage.

Instead, the next card showed a bound woman, blinded and surrounded by knives. Things were only getting worse. Celeste flipped the eighth card and they both gasped when

Death appeared, a silent skeleton riding towards a crimson moon rising over the castle that had once promised a happy home.

"Holy Mother of Jesus," said Mrs. X, glancing at the faded Madonna print hanging above Celeste.

Think quick, Celeste. You can still save this.

"Now, now. This is just emphasizing that it's time for a change—it underlines the explosive image of the Tower."

"Exactly. It's time for me to move back to Missouri and pursue my passion as a water-skiing showgirl," said Mrs. X.

Celeste had heard all about Mrs. X's water-skiing on the Lake of the Ozarks. That's where Mr. X had first spotted her, dressed like Superwoman and sailing behind a motorboat, her black hair shimmering in the midwestern heat. He'd cut a lucrative land deal and secured his aqua superstar that day in the Show Me state.

Luna yowled in protest that her breakfast bowl was empty. But the cupboards were bare and unless Celeste steered Mrs. X back towards her marriage, they'd remain so. She flipped over the penultimate card and breathed a sigh of relief at the visage of a friendly, mustachioed man and his loyal hound. "Strength. That's what you need right now. Strength. To put the past behind you and build back even stronger," she said.

"Or cut loose!" said Mrs. X, as she impatiently turned the last card over herself to find a heart pierced by three swords.

"Oh, my!" yelped Celeste.

Celeste knew Mrs. X was well-versed enough in the cards that she could see what this foretold. Mr. X had stabbed her in the heart multiple times, romance-wise. It would take some strength to walk away from the dream of her marriage—and all the security Mr. X's oil money could buy. But if she moved to Missouri, she'd take her wounded heart and her lucrative patronage with her. That would also be the death of The Happy Heart.

Celeste scanned the cards for a possible way out of this dilemma. To stall a moment longer, she placed both hands in front of her and bowed her head further, as though she were wishing Mrs. X "namaste."

Should she tell Mrs. X she should upend her life just as the cards had revealed? Or should she twist their meaning to secure the status quo? She'd already laid the groundwork for a favorable interpretation, saying that the Tower and Death cards were about a new beginning within the marriage, not without. But that blasted heart pierced by the three swords that appeared at the end? Well, she could argue that it meant Mrs. X should hold fast to the love she had. But she knew that was a lie, and that made Celeste feel like she wasn't just grounded in mud; she was rolling around in it like a prevaricating pig.

The maddening thing was that Celeste had never let her conscience weigh her down before. But today, she felt as pinned by compassion as that pierced heart.

She raised her head and opened her eyes to see Mrs. X weeping into the tails of her mermaid scarf.

Get a hold of yourself, Celeste. This wealthy woman deserved some happiness in life. If she told her the truth, Mrs. X would receive a nice divorce settlement from Mr. X. Enough to afford the long-distance charges if Celeste did readings over the telephone. Telling Mrs. X what the cards had so clearly laid out could be in her best interest after all.

Celeste opened her mouth to do so just as Mrs. X threw her hands into the air and inadvertently knocked over the ambergris candle burning near her elbow. Before she could right it, the flames in the Tower card sprung to life.

Celeste yanked the drooping roses she'd snagged from the day-old cart at the Co-Op out of a Ganesh-shaped vase and threw the remaining water onto the flames.

Both women looked at the sodden mess that remained on the table. Mrs. X wailed even louder.

"Disaster. It's all a disaster. If I stay, I'll lose what little dignity I have. If I leave, I'll be a penniless pauper."

"What?" said Celeste. "Surely Mr. X would provide an ample settlement in the case of... a more permanent separation." She dared not utter the D word.

"That's just it," said Mrs. X. "He made me sign a prenuptial agreement that made sure I'd receive nothing if I ever left him."

"Is that legal?"

"Pretty sure it is. Mr. X is nothing if not protective of his money and how he uses it to control others. Especially me."

At the mention of money, Celeste thought about all the bills resting under a chipped hunk of amethyst on her kitchen table. Without the patronage of Mrs. X, she and Luna would be out on the street. She needed Mrs. X as much as Mrs. X needed her devilish husband.

Celeste bundled the ruined cards and dead roses up in the singed piece of velvet. "Come with me," she said as she marched out the door and into the waiting world.

"But I, you... where are we going?" said Mrs. X.

"Out," said Celeste, not entirely certain herself where she was headed, besides to the garbage bin on the corner. At first Mrs. X hesitated, but then she grabbed her dark glasses and strode after her in her high-heeled Frye boots. Celeste wished she'd put on something more elegant than the worn-out lavender Birkenstocks that matched the purple leotard under her caftan. But then, she hadn't expected to bolt onto the streets with a water-skiing socialite in her wake.

She'd tossed her past—and likely her future—away, when Paolo glided up to dump an empty cup from Yogurt Park. She caught a whiff of something fruity emanating from his long, wavy locks. Or was that the last drops of Mango Tango on his breath?

"Good day, ladies," he said with a bow.

"Mornin' Paul-o," said Celeste, who knew this paisley prince was really Paul from Boise, transported to Berkeley by the university's quest for diversity. A boy from an Idaho potato farm had fit the bill.

Paolo didn't flinch at the snipe. Just sidled up to Mrs. X. He knew a damsel in distress when he saw one.

"Hi there, pretty lady. How can I help?"

Celeste groaned. Now she'd really done it. Whether Mrs. X stayed with or left her cheating husband, she'd never forgive Celeste for exposing her to this street hustler in the guise of a medieval poet.

Mrs. X slipped her dark frames down to regard Paolo.

"You ever water-ski?" she asked.

Paolo's face lit up with an enormous grin.

"Have I ever!"

"Barcelona, Malta, Tarifa?"

"Something like that. Lucky Peak."

Mrs. X squinted, sizing up this potential swain. Celeste stepped in front of Paulo and pleaded with Mrs. X. "Let's return to The Happy Heart—try again with some runes?"

"I think I've seen enough of the future today," said Mrs. X. "I want to live in the moment." She turned to Paolo. "Let's go down to the Berkeley Marina and ski a round or two."

Paolo didn't blink. "Far out!"

"We'll need swimsuits. Let's go," said Mrs. X.

Paolo grinned and extended his arm. Mrs. X ignored his

THE HAPPY HEART

invitation and strode in the direction of the parking lot where she'd stashed her burnt orange BMW.

The initial shock that her best client had been snatched by a bell-bottomed imposter froze Celeste in place at first, but then she rallied to scramble after them.

"Mrs. X, Paul-O!" she cried, breaking into what the young kids called a "jog." "Wait!"

"Oh, Celeste," said Mrs. X, turning to take her in. "I'd nearly forgotten you were here."

Celeste gasped for breath. She really must do more Sun Salutations and fewer Corpse poses. She shot Paolo her best "scram" look. "Let's return to my place. I'll make you a nice cup of tea. We can read the leaves after."

"And forgo my heart's desire?" Mrs. X opened the door and leaned over to release the lock that would allow Paolo to jump in on the other side. She stuck her head out the window. "But you're welcome to join us."

Celeste didn't know how to water-ski and didn't fancy swimming in the cold water straight from the Bay. She thought about heading back to pack up her things; at the very least, feed Luna. Then the fog broke, and a ray of sun hit the chrome fender, nearly blinding her.

She thought she heard her mother's voice saying to seize the moment. "Gladys, you may not be the shiniest tool in the shed, but you can still be the sturdiest one."

"All right," said Celeste, climbing in the back seat and holding on for dear life as Mrs. X sped up Telegraph past Caffe Med. What she wouldn't give for some eggs and hash browns right now.

Mrs. X turned left at the campus border towards Shattuck Avenue. She pulled up in front of Hinks department store and dashed inside with Paolo at her heels. Celeste couldn't see how to open the back door, so she stayed put, fuming and shivering as the fog returned to swirl around the car. If she could have extricated herself, she'd have headed across the street to Edy's for some Lakeshore Tea or maybe—despite the chill—a strawberry milkshake. Taken some back to Luna to make up for the delayed breakfast.

It was as though she were trapped in a Twilight Zone of her own making. When her first attempt at independence—the move north, a job that suited her skills—had proved disappointing, she'd tried to replicate her mother's career. She'd thought she could move out of her comfort zone, but that hadn't been the case. She'd hoped to be a Mary Richards, when in truth, she was at best a Rhoda Morgenstern.

At last, Mrs. X and Paolo returned, swinging a Hinks bag between them. They popped into the car and Mrs. X made an illegal U-turn to take them to University Avenue. She lit up a cigarette and took a long drag before hanging one arm out the window. Doing her best not to cough, Celeste rolled down her window and waved smoke out even as the fog rushed in.

Just as Mrs. X screeched into the lot at Aquatic Park, her headscarf escaped, and it was only Celeste's quick lunge out the window that kept it from blowing into the lagoon. Half-trapped by the still-locked door, she clutched her watery prize. "Your scarf!"

"Keep it," said Mrs. X as she turned back to unlock the door. Then she and Paolo made for a small red boathouse that resembled a floating chicken coop, flanked by two docks. Celeste stumbled after them, repulsed by the fishy smell of the bay.

She tied the scarf around her own hennaed curls and stared out at the lagoon dotted with red buoys. Mrs. X emerged from the changing rooms in a surprisingly prim navy blue one-piece. Paolo joined her, sporting what looked like a pair of men's briefs, Day-Glo yellow and boldly displaying what her mother would have called "the family jewels." They sauntered down to the dock where a man wearing a skipper's cap waited in a speedboat.

You'd think a girl growing up in L.A. would be part mermaid, but Celeste had always been nervous around large bodies of water. For one thing, she tended to freckle and burn. Then there was the time she nearly drowned while her mother was practicing pinup stances on a pier for a photographer beau. She'd decided then, it was best to keep firmly planted on land.

The skipper handed Mrs. X and Paolo two pairs of fat wooden skis. They gamely put them on. Then he picked up the ski ropes like a cowboy twirling a lariat and threw both handles their way. Paolo caught them and gallantly handed one to Mrs. X.

"Hey, climb aboard. I need a spotter." The skipper pointed at Celeste.

"Oh, no, not me. You all go have your fun."

"Lady, did you hear me? I need a spotter to make sure your pals are safe out on the water. Get in."

Now, wasn't that a fine kettle of fish? For Mrs. X to believe she could make her dreams come true right here in her marriage, Celeste would need to navigate the rocking dock, board the bucking boat, and "spot" her best client. She gulped as the skipper stuck out his hairy hand and dragged her aboard.

"Sit there," he said, pointing to the back-facing seat.

Celeste did as she was told, placing the bright orange life jacket over her head and staring straight at Mrs. X and Paolo. She didn't look down. No need to become any more familiar with the brackish water than need be.

"Here, hold this." The skipper passed her a small, striped flag and instructed her to wave it if either of his skiers fell. "And make sure you yell that they're down as well! Don't want to circle round and run over 'em."

Celeste gasped.

He put the boat into gear and slowly crawled away from the shore until Mrs. X shouted, "hit it!" Then he shifted into high gear and took off so suddenly that Celeste nearly fell overboard. The mermaid scarf slipped from her head and, for the third time, she rescued it before it sailed away.

This time, she fastened it securely around her neck as she stared at the two outrageously attractive skiers gliding over the sparkling water. Paolo was strong and fearless as he cut in and out of the wake, but it was Mrs. X who lit up the lagoon.

For the first time since she'd walked into Celeste's place, her client wasn't scurrying so no one could see her, head tucked to avoid others' eyes. "Whoo-hoo!" she cried, raising one fist to the sky as she expertly navigated the racing course marked by bobbing buoys.

If asked about it, Celeste would have insisted it was the sun that caused her eyes to water, not the sight of Mrs. X in all her glory.

On the seventh circle back to the dock, Mrs. X and Paolo released their ropes and sailed hand-in-hand to the shore. The skipper made a hard left and then idled the boat, pulling in one rope as he ordered Celeste to retrieve the other.

"You want to give it a go?" he asked. Celeste looked at him in horror. "Skiing, I mean."

"Oh, that would be far, far out of my comfort zone. I have no capacity for staying afloat."

"That's what these are for." The skipper tugged on her life

jacket. "Probably got some suits over in the Lost & Found bin you could use."

Celeste was no stranger to dumpster diving, but she shuddered thinking about what one might find in the Aquatic Park bin.

Still, the day had grown warm, and the water looked so inviting. She could just strip down to her purple leotard. After all, Mrs. X and Paul-o had made it seem so easy. An image of the doused Tower card appeared to Celeste. "Why not?"

She shucked off her caftan just as a wave hit the dock and soaked her to her knees. She tied the scarf firmly around her waist and let Paolo help her put the skis on before she thudded to a seated position.

"You'll never get up from the dock," said Paulo.

"But you and Mrs. X did."

"Not the first time I skied," he said. "Come in the water with me."

"No way."

Paolo jumped in and dragged her with him. She screamed at the cold, briny bath, as well as the sensation of Paolo holding her in his wiry arms. "Keep your tips up, relax, and lean back," he cried. Hmm. She wondered how many times he'd used that line.

The skipper yelled back, "Ready?"

She'd never be ready. But what did she have to lose?

"Hit it?" she squeaked. The heavy wooden skis sunk beneath the water and her arms were nearly yanked out of their sockets as she belly-flopped forward. She came up sputtering, ready to march back to The Happy Heart in her water-soaked Birks, pack up the trunk with the heart-shaped lock, and post a "For Sale" sign. But then Paolo was suddenly at her side, encouraging her to give it another go, promising he'd stay with her for as long as it took. Try after try, he kept his word, fitting her feet back into the ski bindings even as her stubby legs trembled from exertion.

Meanwhile, Mrs. X shouted encouragement from the back of the boat. "You can do this, Celeste! It's in the cards!"

Celeste summoned up all the guiding spirits she'd ever fabricated for her clients and asked them to grant her this wish: for once, let her not be grounded, but instead take flight.

A gull flew over and squawked directly into her ear, drowning out Mrs. X's cheers just as the boat shot forward. Eureka! She was up! Though she still shook like a terrified squid, bent nearly double and legs splayed, she nevertheless skimmed across the lagoon, the tails of the mermaid scarf sailing behind her.

Her element would never be water—or fire, if this morning's candle disaster was any indication—but for now, she'd left the muddy earth and all its concerns behind. She was flying, a creature of the air, just like her mother. She hollered back to the gull what Paul-o had yelled as she jetted away from his arms: "Far out!"

Kathryn Pritchett writes about strong women forged in the American West—including the People's Republic of Berkeley! She's currently looking for representation for her debut novel *The Casket Maker's Other Wife*, a fictionalized account of her great-great-grandmother's polygamous marriage set in late 19th century Utah and Idaho Territories. Her WIP, *To See the Love-Light*, features Gilded Age actress Maude Adams, Broadway's original Peter Pan. Visit Kathryn's website at ThingsElemental.com and follow her on Facebook, Instagram and Twitter.

TRUST NO ONE
BY ANA BRAZIL

WASHINGTON D.C., FEBRUARY 1943

Eunice folded me into a bear hug as soon as I stepped through the portal of the Passenger Concourse at Union Station. For a petite woman, she had a long reach and a tight squeeze.

"I thought the Boston train would never arrive." She released me and immediately inspected my gloved hands. "Trudy! Where's your overnight bag?"

"I'm not staying the night."

Eunice frowned, as though I couldn't be trusted to follow her directions. "You did bring a present, didn't you? Something for the mother-to-be?"

"I did." I pulled a brown-paper parcel from my coat pocket.

"Oh, no," Eunice winced. "It's not a book, is it?"

"Babies don't like books?"

"Yes, they do, eventually. But a stork shower is for more

practical things. Bonnets and blankies. Diapers. That sort of thing."

"It's a very good book," I insisted. "It's even got an illustration at the front."

"Never mind." Eunice took my arm as we plunged through a crush of uniformed Army men making for the train platforms. "And don't worry that it's not wrapped properly. I'm sure I have some extra ribbon."

Instead of joining the slow-moving taxi line beneath the entrance portico, Eunice led me across the street to Columbus Circle and an elegant 1940 Packard coupe. The car was so impeccably clean and shiny, I almost whistled in appreciation.

"Since when does the Colonel let you drive his car?" The Colonel—her current and my former boss—had never let me drive his Packard, even though my father had the same car, and he had let me drive anywhere in our Beacon Hill neighborhood.

"The Colonel insisted."

"Why? Does he still think the District's a hotbed of German spies? That if we take a taxi or a bus we'll be captured and tortured to reveal every OSS secret in the book?" I plucked a stray leaf from the front windshield and let it float to the ground. "Still a careful old prick, isn't he?"

"Trudy! Language!"

It wasn't the first time I'd shocked Eunice with my plain talking, and just like before, I replied quickly, in a voice only she could hear, "*Immer noch ein vorsichtiges altes Schwanz, richtig?*"

It took her a few seconds to understand my translation. "Nope! It doesn't sound any better in German."

We slipped into the car, which smelled heavily of the Colonel's Lucky Strike cigarettes. Eunice tapped the gas pedal —careful not to grind her shoe heels into the floorboard— turned on the ignition, and hit the starter button. "But you're right, the Colonel is a careful old bird. *Trust no one*, and all that."

As she eased away from the curb and onto the ever-crowded Massachusetts Avenue, I sensed something different about Eunice. She'd exchanged her well-worn gray beret for a more fashionable black fedora, and she seemed to have more confidence, more self-assurance. She even seemed taller than her five-feet, one-inch. So much taller that I glanced to where her bottom hit the coupe's seat, wondering if she had a cushion hidden beneath her. She didn't.

"Can you blame him?" Eunice returned to talking about the Colonel. "He's the second highest officer in America's spy agency"—which is what everyone working at the Office of Strategic Services called the OSS. "Of course, he's careful. And deliberate. And strategic."

I couldn't disagree. Everything Eunice said about the Colonel was true, except she'd omitted that he was also one untrustworthy son-of-a-bitch.

The Colonel had been a Harvard classmate of my father's and had dined often at our house over the last thirty years, always praising me for my ambition and cleverness. When the war started, he immediately recruited me to work for him in Washington, promising to give my talents full rein. Instead, he assigned me to filing purchase orders in a closet. All day long.

When he finally allowed me to enroll in his first training course for female agents, he criticized my contributions and denied my successes. He was wrong, of course. Because I was not only smarter than the other four trainees, I was more focused, more deliberate, and more willing to do whatever was needed to achieve my goal.

Today, I was going to prove that.

Eunice and I drove in silence for a few blocks, me looking

from side to side at the monumental stone buildings lining the street; Eunice keeping her eyes on the cars and taxis in front of us. Eunice became so intent on navigating the traffic on Massachusetts Avenue that I took over the conversation.

"The Colonel *is* at home today, isn't he?"

"He is. Despite it being Saturday."

A snowflake hit the windshield. It had been cold and cloudy when I left Boston, but this was the first actual flake. Eunice saw it too and pouted, as though her delicate scowl could postpone the snow until we reached the Colonel's house. Or what used to be the Colonel's house, because once the war started and the world came to Washington and housing in the District became impossible, the Colonel offered his majestic family mansion to the fourteen girls working for him as typists and clerks at the OSS. Girls that, at the time, included me.

"He's home," said Eunice suddenly, "and he wants to see you."

That was perfect, because I wanted to see him, too. I'd told Mother that I needed to come to Washington for a stork shower, but my real mission was to confront the Colonel. I hadn't told Eunice that, of course, because she was right about one thing: *trust no one.*

Traffic thinned as we ventured into the Embassy Row blocks of Massachusetts Avenue, and we had a lane to ourselves and room to look around. But, despite the impressive display of international flags and sentries guarding the embassies, my thoughts remained on the Colonel.

"He wants to see me about the job, doesn't he?" *Courier to occupied France. The first field job for an OSS woman.* The job I wanted more than anything in the world. The job I'd earned through those six weeks in the Colonel's training program. The job that the Colonel inexplicably bestowed on Izzie, today's mother-to-be.

Losing that job to Izzie had embarrassed me; infuriated me; crushed me. I'd left Washington within hours of the rejection, and had been living with my parents ever since. But now that Izzie's pregnancy disqualified her for service, I'd returned to Washington to demand the Colonel send me to France.

I'd also demanded that Eunice prepare the Colonel for my return. "You did remind him I was the smartest girl in class, didn't you? Like you said you would?"

Eunice slid the car into a spot directly in front of the Colonel's house. "You're my best friend ever, Trudy. The best roommate a woman could have." She busied herself with turning the car off and setting the brake before continuing, "Of course, I put in a word for you."

She looked directly at me for a few seconds, her mouth open as if she was about to say something. As if she thought I didn't believe her, she raised her right hand to her shoulder in the Girl Scouts's salute. "I swear it, Trudy."

She looked away quickly and nodded to the Colonel's house and a large window, where we saw a clutch of girls with glasses in their hands. "Let's get you inside. It looks like the party's already started."

I'D HATED IZZIE LANDREW—GRACEFUL, gregarious, gorgeous mother-to-be Izzie—since the first day we met. And from the moment the Colonel assigned Izzie *my* behind-the-lines-in-France courier job, I'd been toying with ways to kill her.

And then, a month ago, in the midst of her final phase of advanced training, Izzie had been forced to confess that she'd gotten married a year ago, and she was now pregnant. Seeing Izzie in her pregnancy misery—her swollen face and fingers, the perspiration dotting her forehead, the handkerchief clutched to her mouth—I still wanted to kill her. Not for stealing my job, but for being so irresponsible. How could she give up the opportunity to use her training in devastated, dependent France? How could she turn her back on making this horrendous war end sooner? How could she sacrifice her moment of glory in the field for a baby?

Izzie waddled toward me in uneven, awkward steps, last Christmas's plaid party dress straining across her protruding belly. "Hello, Trudy. The girls and I were wondering if you'd bother to show up."

Girls. How I hated being called that. But no matter which of the Seven Sisters we had graduated from, or that some of us had been professionally employed before joining the OSS, or that some of us were into our thirties, the Colonel called us girls. *His* girls. Even worse, we called ourselves *the Colonel's girls*.

And today, all fourteen of the Colonel's girls were in his parlor, an impressively cozy and warm room off his entrance hall. Yes, all of his current girls were dressed in their most fabulous party clothes, enjoying his fire, playing his records, drinking his booze, and as always, keeping their distance from me.

Except for Eunice, who parked herself between me and Izzie and hooked her arms into both of ours.

"Izzie, why don't you join Clara on the sofa? And Trudy"—Eunice dazzled me with her peacemaking smile—"Can you help me pass out the paper and pens? It's time for the games to begin."

UNLOCKED

TEN MINUTES later I eased away from a heated debate about baby feeding times. I slipped out of the parlor and moved lightly across the majestic entrance hall to the Colonel's library. I took a moment to refresh my lipstick in the hall mirror; it was *Victory Red*, the Elizabeth Arden shade Eunice and I both wore. After wiping a speck of color from my front teeth, I entered the library without knocking, determined to confront the Colonel before he could speak.

But the Colonel wasn't at his desk, wasn't anywhere in the room.

I entered anyway, because if there was one room in the Colonel's mansion that I missed, it was his exquisite library. Paneled in exotic woods, furnished with comfortable chairs and Aubusson rugs, the library boasted thousands of books. Biographies, chronicles, journals, maps, and even novels, the Colonel's library had it all.

It also housed dozens of carefully curated relics and *objets d'art*, all speaking to the Colonel's travels and connections. An inkwell used by John Hancock, a chair from Abraham Lincoln's White House, and, most recently, a starling stuffed by a young Franklin Roosevelt—these treasures and more were given places of honor amongst the books.

My favorite relic was an old wooden chest the size of a picnic hamper. Dark and footed and worn down by centuries of use, the chest still had a faint outline of a heart carved on the front.

The lock on the chest was heart-shaped also, but the key had been lost long ago. Finding a way to unlock that cranky combination of rusted metal had been the Colonel's first field test for me, and I had succeeded in record time.

I'd been thrilled to pick the lock and open the chest, suspecting that my eyes would be the first in decades to view the insides. Instead, I'd found a letter inside addressed to me. From the Colonel, of course, commanding me to get back to work.

This afternoon, the chest lid opened readily, revealing three cartons of Lucky Strikes, quite the cache during wartime. But I had no time for a smoke; no time for the sentiment of memory; not when I had a job to do.

The Colonel's private suite was on the second floor, the last room down the corridor from his grand staircase. From the cigarette odor wafting around his door, I knew he was inside. I knocked, heard his "Come in," and entered.

The odors hit me first. Vomit. Urine. Shit. The stink might all be coming from the Colonel's small bathroom at the end of his suite, but it was too close for comfort.

I'd expected to see him working at the small desk in the corner, but instead, the Colonel was in bed, propped up by stiff pillows and weighed down with two cotton quilts. His striped flannel pajamas looked three sizes too large for him, exposing his bruised, boney neck and a scraggle of gray hair on his chest. He hadn't shaved for days, and the white bristle made his face look even paler. In the months that I'd been gone, he'd aged from a hale-and-hearty fifty-five-years-old to… I wasn't sure.

For a man named after Rough Rider Teddy Roosevelt, the Colonel's sudden deterioration was hard to reconcile. Here was a man who'd been—like Colonel Roosevelt—endlessly, almost obnoxiously healthy. The Colonel's invalid appearance stopped me cold, and it was moments before I found my voice.

"What's wrong with you?" I repressed the inclination to finish the sentence with a respectful *Sir*, something I'd always done in the past.

"That's my Trudy." His words were slow and low. "Straight and to the point. Small talk be damned."

Without warning, a spittle of blood bubbled from between his lips. He coughed, a crusty burst that ripped from his chest, tore through his throat and seemed to last forever. When it finally finished, he wiped his mouth with his handkerchief and pushed the cloth onto the bedside table to his right. Already covered with an array of hospital equipment and bottles, a pack of Lucky Strikes and a saucer of cigarette butts and ashes, the bedside table refused the handkerchief and it fell to the rug.

The Colonel'd long ago exhausted any of my sympathies, but still, I was curious. "What is it?" And yes, I was bitter. "Some type of venereal disease?"

He blanched, as though I'd guessed correctly. So I kept at it, assured that since I'd never slept with him, my own health was not at risk.

"Is it syph? Is your bayonet falling off?" I lingered a little on the soldier's word for their cock. "Is that why you're so pale?"

"Diabetes." He spit as he spoke, fumbling through his pajama pocket for another handkerchief. "It's killing me."

"It's not supposed to kill you." All of us in the house knew about the Colonel's struggle with diabetes and the insulin he took throughout the day to control it. "Not if you take care of yourself."

"Maybe it's not the diabetes." He took his time retrieving an already-burning cigarette from the saucer on his bedside table. "Does it matter? I'm dying. I thought you'd be happy."

Happy? No, that wasn't why my stomach was churning,

why I wanted to run to the Colonel's bathroom, even though the stench from it grew more noxious. It was frustration. Because if anyone put the Colonel into his grave, I wanted it to be me.

He nodded to the chair that was already pointed toward him. "Sit there, so I can see you."

I removed a wilted cushion from the chair, clutched it in front of me, and sat.

The Colonel stabbed out his cigarette and fumbled with a pack of Lucky Strikes before finding another. He pushed it deep between the index and third fingers of his right hand, anchoring it hard, so it wouldn't budge. He nodded at the carton and I took a smoke for myself. I lit both our cigarettes with his monogrammed lighter.

The Colonel took his time inhaling. He also took his time studying his cigarette before addressing me. "I have a job for you, Trudy."

I squashed my cigarette in his saucer. *The courier job.* Finally. Even though the Colonel must know how much I wanted this job, that I was bursting with excitement, I replied as coolly as I could. "I'm listening."

The Colonel replied just as coolly. "Trudy, I want you to kill me."

Now I was certain the Colonel had a venereal disease. An advanced case of VD that was invading his mind and body. Because the Colonel I knew would never concede defeat; he always had a trick or two up his sleeve.

"You want me to kill you?"

"I do. And I want you to do it today. Now." His head turned

toward the window, as though he could look outside, although I realized his body didn't angle that far.

I forced myself to humor him. "Aren't you dying anyway?"

"Not fast enough, and what I have doesn't end gently. I want no part of it."

I remembered watching my grandmother die from a mass of tumors. Her passing had been long and pitiless, and I would have done anything to make it easier for her. Anything.

"You can't do it yourself, can you?" I'd watched him wince when he stuffed his cigarette between his fingers. "Because something's happened to your hand."

"Something, indeed," he replied. "Enough something that I can't hold a syringe steady. I certainly can't plunge it."

"But why me? You've got thirteen other girls in this house."

"Because you hate me, Trudy. You're the only person I know who really wants me dead."

"I'm not the only person who hates you." I thought of the stories of seduction and manipulation I'd overheard in the house and at the office. "At least three of the girls downstairs—or their boyfriends and fathers—would be glad to kill you."

"But you hate me the most." The Colonel seemed to relish our mutual bluntness. "Don't you?"

I certainly expected I hated him the most, a hatred that had grown deeper and angrier since I quit the OSS. I hated him more this very moment, for being sick and weak and looking for an easy way out.

"I have reason to hate you. You pulled a nasty trick on me. First telling me I was a shoo-in for the courier position and then giving it to Izzie. I aced every test you gave me."

And I had. From jury-rigging broken radios to surviving the freezing wilderness overnight to unlocking that damn chest, I'd beaten every girl in my training class. Izzie and Eunice, Joan and Clara. None of them were as good as me.

And then it hit me. Maybe the Colonel's pallor and thinness, his raspy voice and shaking hands, even the dried blood around his mouth was all a test?

I snatched the largest bottle from his bedside table. It was a generic *Expectorant Compound for Coughs*, with the Colonel's name penciled on the label. Half-empty, it certainly looked real. I removed the cap; it smelled real too.

Ever so slowly, the Colonel grabbed a bottle from his table with his left hand and tossed it onto the cushion in my lap. These contents were not so generic: *Potion AB8 Experiment 7* and *Prepared by the Department of Laboratories, Army Medical School*. Now I knew the Colonel must be really sick, to be taking one of the DOL's experimental potions.

"I might have four weeks to live," he said. "Four weeks of fighting for breath, forgetting my name, and shitting in my bed."

At the mention of his bodily functions, this all seemed real. But still I had to ask, "This isn't another test? Like parachuting into a tree? To see how I make field decisions, or something like that?"

"Not a test, although there is a prize of sorts. If you succeed."

"I... I get a *prize* for killing you?"

"A prize, reward... whatever you like to call it."

Maybe this wasn't a test after all. With a prize to be won, maybe this was really a *game*.

"Here's the deal, Trudy." The Colonel's watery gray eyes held my full attention. "Kill me now, and the courier position is yours."

The courier position is yours. The exact words I wanted to hear. I tapped down the smile curling at the end of my lips. Whether this was a test or a game, this was precisely where I needed to be most careful.

"How would this all happen?" I asked as clinically as I could. "Me killing you?"

The Colonel had been tilting precariously toward me, as if he wanted to reach out, take me by the shoulders, and shake me until I did his bidding. But now, something seemed to relax within him, like a spring had been released. Like he knew he had me.

He lowered himself against his pillows. "Inside my top drawer is enough insulin to kill me twice over."

I opened the drawer, expecting it contained anything except insulin. But the small brown case holding both the Colonel's syringe and insulin ampules was already open and the contents ready for the taking. Included in the case was another glass syringe, almost twice as big as the Colonel's usual, with the needle already attached.

"That one," he wrenched his neck to look into the drawer. "Draw those two ampules of insulin into that large bastard, and then you can kill me."

I stared at the insulin kit, struggling to understand. The Colonel's exchange—his death for my courier job—sounded too good to be true.

"How is this going to work? If you're dead"—I paused reflectively, as though respectfully mourning his passing—"how do I get the job?"

"I left a letter for the Chief in the library. Recommending you for the position."

"*Recommending*?" We both knew that the Chief—William Donovan, head of the OSS—balked at sending women into occupied France. With the Chief so resistant, what good was a dead man's recommendation? I didn't need a recommendation; I needed a champion.

"*Highly* recommending," the Colonel added. "It's the most I could do for you, dead or alive. If it works, you could be in England before the end of the week."

I ran my finger along the glass barrel of the largest syringe, confused that there were no markings on it.

"It's the most I could do," he repeated. "The rest is up to you."

"Fine." I picked up the syringe and—just as I'd been trained—tested the needle to make sure it was secure. Then I examined the tip to make sure it was sharp. It was. "Where in your library is the letter?"

"In that old chest you were so fond of."

"But I already—"

"Under the false bottom," he interrupted. "Which I'm guessing you didn't already open."

No, I hadn't, and I wanted to kick myself for not dislodging the cigarette cartons and looking under the false bottom. I knew I should put down the syringe and race to the library to make sure there actually was a letter under the false bottom, but I was too captivated by the possibilities of death by insulin.

"If I inject you with"—I looked at the insulin ampule label and multiplied it by two—"eighty units of insulin, you'll die quickly? Within minutes?"

"Seconds. I'll be dead before you leave the room." He responded matter-of-factly, but his eyes went suddenly soft.

I continued to talk myself through it. "Then I wipe my fingerprints from the syringe, needle, and ampule. And the drawer knob. And anything else I've touched while in here." I glanced about the room, identifying exactly what I'd touched. Would the fabric on the wilted cushion retain fingerprints? I didn't know. And would my cigarette—stubbed out in the Colonel's saucer—work against me or—

"No need to worry about fingerprints on anything." He seemed to read my thoughts. "No one will suspect anything."

His voice took on a new energy, as though there was a real possibility his pain would end soon. "Not many people know this, but insulin is just about the perfect murder weapon."

"It'll leave an injection mark," I told him.

"I've got so many that one more won't draw anyone's suspicion. And even if someone suspected an insulin overdose, coroners have no test for it."

I'd learned plenty about poisons, but nothing about insulin. Except now I knew what kept the Colonel alive could also kill him. And if it could kill *him*, it should kill anyone. That is, if I could trust what he was telling me.

"Once you're dead"—this time as I mentioned his death, I did not respectfully pause—"I'll go down to the library, collect your recommendation, and deliver it to the Chief."

"He'll be in the office from four until six today."

We both looked at his bedside clock. It was almost three now, so I had one hour before the Chief would be in his office. "But the Chief needs to know you're dead by then. The recommendation is only important if you're dead."

"I've asked Izzie to check on me at a quarter to four. If I'm dead when she comes up, her first call will be to the Chief. If I'm not dead—"

"The letter is no good to me anyway."

The Colonel had thought it through, all right.

"Get to it, Trudy." The Colonel twitched from pain as he spoke, making it easy to imagine how miserable the next weeks of his life could be: his mind softening, his bowels loosening, his entire body attacking him. There'd be no escaping his pain, especially since most morphine and other pain killers were kept in reserve for military use.

That's when I wanted to know, "What happens if I don't kill you?"

"You'll be finished in Washington," he answered quickly. "If you ever thought you could get another war job, or convince another officer to place you anywhere... well, that will never happen."

I'd been expecting him to detail his pain, perhaps even beg me to end his life, and his threats chilled me. I'd heard the sad stories of other government girls who'd taken one wrong step, lost their jobs, and fled home to Ohio or Maine. Sure, I'd gone home to Boston when I left the OSS, but I hadn't been fired.

"You have to do it today," he rasped out. "Or else Eunice is on the first transport to England tomorrow morning."

"Eunice?" Had he really said her name? Or was his mind failing him already?

Suddenly, the mighty insulin didn't interest me anymore. Eunice did. She'd begged me to be her roommate so we could study together. She'd called me her best friend ever. And now she'd stolen my job.

"You picked Eunice after Izzie turned up pregnant? You picked Eunice over me?"

"Eunice will make an excellent—"

Eunice had sworn to convince the Colonel that I should have the courier job, and her betrayal overwhelmed me. I looked down at the syringe of insulin in my hand and couldn't stop thinking about Eunice. "I've always been better than Eunice, and you know it."

"Better at what, Trudy? Hesitating? Because all I see is that you can't make a damn decision."

But I had made a decision. And it was all so easy now that I had eighty units of insulin in my hand. First, I'd kill the Colonel, and then I'd kill Eunice.

Why not? The Colonel had claimed insulin was almost the perfect murder weapon. If eighty units of insulin would kill the Colonel—who I guessed was down to one hundred and twenty pounds—it would certainly kill Eunice, who weighed much less.

I slid the needle into the first ampule and drew the insulin into the syringe. I did the same for the second ampule, satisfied to see the syringe almost full.

I placed the syringe upon the cushion from my chair and moved to the Colonel's bedside.

"I'm ready now," I announced. "Is there any—"

"No."

"Where—"

"My stomach."

I removed the two pillows supporting his back and he eased down toward the mattress, almost turning onto his side as if to take a nap. When he was flat on his back, he pulled down his bedding and lifted up his pajama top. He lowered his bottoms slightly and while he struggled to expose his lower abdomen, I took the syringe from the cushion and put it on his table.

Then with both hands, just as he saw I wasn't holding the syringe anymore, I leaned over him and forced the cushion into his face. I refused him any air, grinding the fine feathers into his nose and mouth.

His arms flailed up at me, his thin fingers grasping for anything they could. I kept pressing. He scratched at my sleeve with his fingernails. I kept pressing. He tried to raise his knees, move his legs, kick his feet, but his bed covers frustrated him.

I pressed so hard on the Colonel's face that my palms

scuffed against his brow. So hard the small bones in my hands tingled and the slats under his bed groaned. I was quick and efficient, just as I always determined to be. I even kept breathing steadily, slowly, making sure to give myself the air I was denying him.

He stopped fighting; he went slack; but I kept pressing. And then I counted to sixty. And sixty again. I removed the cushion from his face and examined it—ready to clean up any blood, drool, or snot I found; something they never taught us in class. The cushion looked innocent enough, as did the Colonel's face. Well, almost. I lifted him up and combed his hair. Then I smoothed his eyebrows into their natural alignment. Assured that he looked like he died in his sleep, I carefully placed the syringe in my pocket.

I took and held a deep breath before stepping into his bathroom, where I wiped off all my lipstick and watched the paper swirl down his toilet.

I HEARD shrieks of laughter the moment I stepped on the grand staircase. The girls were still at their party. While they'd played baby games, I'd killed the Colonel and figured out how to secure the courier job.

First, I'd get the letter from the chest and then, when Eunice stopped the Packard to let me off at Union Station, I'd inject her with the insulin. I'd not only make the injection look like suicide, but I'd refresh Eunice's Victory Red lipstick to connect her to the stained cigarette butt in the Colonel's bedroom. Just in case anyone suspected the Colonel had been murdered.

I entered the library from the side door, the one not visible from the parlor. Just in case any of the girls were sober enough to look across the entrance hall and see me.

I removed the cigarette cartons from the chest and tossed them on the floor. The false bottom was a piece of wood the size of the chest's real bottom, and it hid about two inches of the chest. Perfect for my letter. I pushed one end of the false bottom and the other end lifted so easily I wondered if the Colonel had oiled it before adding my letter.

But my letter wasn't under the false bottom. Nothing was.

I ran my fingertips over every inch of the insides, not because I expected to find the letter, but... what else was I to do? I even searched—vainly—for a second false bottom.

I turned the chest over—seeing nothing stuck under the bottom—and slammed the chest toward the cigarettes. I tore apart everything I saw. No letter for me anywhere.

I'd been right. Venereal disease must have destroyed his brain.

But ever so slowly, I realized the truth. The Colonel's brain hadn't betrayed him. *He'd* betrayed me. He lied to me. Deliberately. He'd never written the Chief a letter, never recommended me for the courier job. Worse than that, he'd used me, playing on my ambitions to get the quick death he wanted, all the while knowing I'd never get what I wanted.

If I hadn't already killed the Colonel, I'd certainly have killed him now.

I POKED my head into the parlor, trying my best to look enthusiastic as the girls played their *Let's Name Baby* game. Once I knew Eunice had seen me, I went to the front door and moved the blackout cloth to look out the window beside it.

She was waiting when I turned around, arms across her chest.

I stated the obvious. "The snow's coming down harder. If I don't start back now, I won't get a train to Boston tonight."

"We've hardly seen you!" Eunice tried to put her arm around my shoulders, as if to drag me back into the party, but I shrunk from her touch, sure if she got any closer she'd notice the outline of the syringe in my pocket.

"I'll call a taxi," I said, knowing Eunice would protest.

She shook herself like the good soldier she was and straightened until she was almost at attention. "Absolutely not. I'll take you."

Exactly the response I expected.

"I've still got the keys in my pocket." She wiggled her fingers in her pocket nervously. "And... and... there's something I want to tell you."

Despite the cold, the Packard started quickly.

With the windshield wiper squeaking the snow away, Eunice started down Massachusetts Avenue. I fussed with the car's heater, clicking it on and off at least twice, just to have something to do. Or maybe to distract myself. Or to prevent myself from searching out the back window to see if anyone was following me. Izzie might follow the Colonel's instructions to check on him at a quarter to four, or she might be knocking on his door right now, surprising him with a slice of cake and a cup of tea. Then again, the Colonel might have lied about Izzie checking on him at all.

I was still fiddling with the heater knobs when Eunice

reached out and touched my hand. "You know, don't you? The Colonel told you he assigned me the courier job?"

She removed her hand to steady the steering wheel, but I kept my hand on the heater knob, refusing to look at her, letting her stew a little, knowing she was the worst at waiting.

"He made me promise not to say anything to you, Trudy. He made me promise." She sniffed and I saw tears pooling in her eyes. "Although sometimes I think those promises are just a game with him."

Of course they were, I wanted to tell her. All the Colonel ever did was give tests, play games, and lie.

"I wanted to tell you, Trudy, but he wouldn't let me. It was an order. He wanted to tell you in person."

She squirmed in her seat, looking nowhere as tall or confident as she had while driving earlier. She twisted toward me, and her skirt rode up her thighs until I saw the tops of her stockings. "This shouldn't change anything between us, Trudy. You'll always be my best friend ever."

When she returned to watch the road, I unbuttoned my coat. I opened it wide and began straightening my dress belt. I put my hand on the pocket with the syringe, lightly touching it under my fingertips. The pocket fabric was dry; the syringe still contained the full eighty units of insulin.

As we neared Columbus Circle and the entrance to Union Station, I said, "No need to park at the station. Not with everyone else trying to get home before the storm." I motioned to a stretch of street without any cars or passersby. "You can drop me here."

She glided into the spot quickly, as if awkwardly eager to make amends. "You're sure this is okay?"

"It's fine."

Eunice set the brake, keeping the car running. I opened my

arms to gather her into one last bear hug, suddenly remembering how fiercely I'd pushed the cushion into the Colonel's face. I wondered if I could smother Eunice in my embrace. If I *should* smother her and save the insulin in case I needed it later.

We held each other for seconds, until I couldn't tell the beating of our hearts apart. Then I slipped the Colonel's needle from my coat pocket.

I clutched her hard against my chest as I plunged the needle into her thigh. Her stocking shredded, her fingers tightened on my shoulder, and she gasped.

"Tru—

Her body grew heavy and dropped into mine. I drew a deep breath, something she'd never do again.

Before I shoved her into a sitting position on the back seat and put the almost-empty needle between her fingers, before I pushed her body over onto the seat so she wouldn't be found for a while, and before I trudged to Union Station and the train to Boston, I whispered in her ear, as if I were still her best roommate, her best friend ever.

"Never forget the Colonel's first lesson, Eunice. *Trust no one.*"

Ana Brazil loves to write and read historical fiction about curious, ambitious, and bodacious women. Set in 1889 New

Orleans, Ana's historical mystery *Fanny Newcomb & The Irish Channel Ripper* won the IBPA Gold for Historical Fiction. Her short stories "Kate Chopin Tussles with a Novel Ending" and "Miss Evelyn Nesbit Presents" have appeared in crime fiction anthologies. Many years ago, Ana inherited the scrapbooks, recordings, and theatrical ephemera of vaudevillian Elsie Clark, and Ana used this treasure trove to create Viola Vermillion, the smart and sassy vaudeville heroine of her work-in-progress, *The Red-Hot Blues Chanteuse*. Join up with Ana at anabrazil.com, Facebook, Twitter, and Instagram.

TRUE LEGACY
BY LINDA ULLESEIT

PORTLAND, OREGON, 1921

The grandeur of the Multnomah Hotel greeted them like ladies of the highest society. At each of the marble and terra cotta columns in the lobby, a bellman waited to help guests with their luggage. Eva straightened her back, repositioned her tiny daughter in her arms, and swept down the length of the carpeted lobby, trying not to strain her neck staring up at the gilt ceiling with its crystal chandeliers, as she followed her Aunt Emily to the front desk.

The stylish but conservatively dressed woman behind the desk gave them the vacant smile she likely used for all the hotel's non-celebrity guests. After all, the Multnomah reigned as the Pacific Northwest's largest and most modern hotel. All manner of important people stayed there. Eva imagined the opulent lifestyle of her great-aunt Nina, who'd lived on the fourth floor of the Multnomah for many years prior to her recent passing. "How may I help you, ladies?" the clerk asked.

"We have come to meet with..." Aunt Emily made a show of retrieving a note from her purse. "Yes, with Miss Marian Fields. She expects me." At the clerk's blank expression, Aunt Emily continued. "Emily Williams from California. Mrs. Nina Larowe was my relative. I believe Miss Fields was a friend of Mrs. Larowe?"

The clerk's face came alive only to fade into sorrow. "I am so sorry for your loss, Miss Williams. Mrs. Larowe was a dear woman. I see you'll be staying in her apartment overnight?" Aunt Emily nodded. "I will have a bellman show you up." The clerk nodded into the space behind the guests, and a bellman appeared.

Eva's daughter fussed in her arms. At six months, she was not impressed by her surroundings. "Shhh, Sheila," Eva murmured. "Only a few more moments." A few more moments before her feeding, and a few more moments before they discovered the reason Miss Fields had summoned them to Portland from San Francisco.

Eva and Aunt Emily followed the bellman into the elevator. They rode to the fourth floor, where the bellman led them to the apartment belonging to Eva's late Great Aunt Nina, whom she had never met. Eva knew only that her family was full of strong women, extraordinary for their times. She was eager to learn more about Nina Larowe and add Nina's story to her growing repertoire of tales for Sheila. Eva found inspiration in these stories of regular women taking control of their lives and succeeding. Too often, her own life seemed inconsequential.

The plush carpeting deepened the hush in the hallway. Gilt frames held landscape paintings that must be of Oregon locales. The bellman knocked on a door and turned to leave.

"Your valises will be sent right up," he said.

A stooped woman opened the door. Her posture and gray

hair identified her as elderly, but her sharp gaze was decades younger. "You must be Miss Williams. I am Marian Fields. Thank you for coming." She raised her eyebrows at Eva and the baby.

"Please, call me Emily. This is my niece, Eva Walters, and her daughter, Sheila."

Miss Fields smiled at all of them and indicated they were to join her in front of the fire. When their train had left San Francisco, spring warmed the air and green buds covered the trees and bushes. In Portland, however, it was gray and cold.

Aunt Emily had lost no time arranging this trip, once she received Miss Fields' letter informing her of Mrs. Larowe's death and asking her to come to Portland. As a result, the apartment remained decorated to the late Nina Larowe's taste. Two brocade sofas with worn, overstuffed upholstery and scratched wooden legs dominated the room. White crown molding and columns flanked the fireplace, and a large mirror with a heavy gilded frame hung above the cluttered mantle. Shelves covering one entire wall were laden with souvenir plates from all over the world. From where Eva sat, she could see one from New York and one from Paris. Curiosity tempted her closer, but propriety kept her seated on the sofa. She turned to look at the photos on the sofa table behind her. Eva recognized Nina, short and dark-haired like most women in the family, and with the figure her grandmother called thick, photographed with her sister and brother, and with older people who had the look of relatives.

Sheila interrupted her inspection, wiggling and fussing. Eva said, "I'm sorry, Miss Fields, but is there a private place where I may nurse my daughter?"

"Of course, dear." She waved toward a doorway.

Eva walked into the bedroom, past a door to a private bath

that completed the suite. She perched on the white hobnail chenille bedspread and proceeded to nurse her very patient six-month-old daughter.

What would it be like to live in a hotel apartment? This was a nice one, but she couldn't imagine living here with Teddy and Sheila, no matter how grand the public rooms of the Multnomah Hotel were. Eva loved the garden at their rented house in Napa. Mrs. Larowe, however, had possessed no husband, no children, and no family, other than the daughter of her stepsister, to deal with the mysterious issue at the heart of Miss Fields' summons. Eva's own presence in Portland, on the invitation of her aunt, had nothing to do with Mrs. Larowe's estate. Eva had come looking for an adventure and to learn about Great-Aunt Nina. It was fitting that Aunt Emily had brought Eva here, since Aunt Emily was the keeper of the family stories.

And what stories they were! Nina's mother had lived a frontier life at Fort Snelling in the Wisconsin Territory. She'd known Zachary Taylor's family before he became president. Eva's grandmother had come around the horn from New York to California with just her sister, wearing scandalous bloomers on the trip and riding a donkey through the Nicaraguan jungle. Other ancestors came over on the *Mayflower*, the *Lyon*, and other early immigrant ships, and later owned newspapers and reading rooms. Aunt Emily had told Eva about these women, and it was Eva's delightful duty to pass them all on to Sheila, and Sheila's children.

With Sheila fed, diaper changed, and once more snuggly, Eva returned to the parlor where Aunt Emily and Miss Fields were deep in conversation. Listening carefully, Eva learned that Aunt Emily, as the departed's closest relative, would receive something from Nina's estate.

"Mrs. Larowe owned the Nob Hill Theater in our town. She

left it to the Oregon Humane Society with instructions to use the proceeds to relieve the suffering of dumb animals." Miss Fields winced. "Her words, not mine. The property is set up in a trust for ten years, with a hundred dollars a month going to the society."

Aunt Emily laughed. "Well, that's a relief. I heard she'd left everything to a cat."

Eva smiled and said, "In a way, she did. Just to a whole lot of cats rather than one."

Aunt Emily shared her smile. Miss Fields did not.

Instead, Miss Fields glanced at a scarred wooden chest with four stubby legs that, some time ago, had been painted black. It was about two feet high and wide, a little longer than it was tall. Intricate carved designs decorated each side, with a heart-shaped lock on the front. It sat at the end of the couch, where Eva guessed it had doubled as a low end table. Now it was bare of doily or decoration.

"I brought you here not to talk about the theater bequest, but to give you an item of importance to my late friend." Miss Fields' voice quivered. She must have cared deeply for Mrs. Larowe. Miss Fields handed Aunt Emily a heavy key. "Nina wanted you to have this chest."

Aunt Emily took the key and said, "It's very old. Do you have any idea where it came from?"

Miss Fields shook her head. "Nina said once that it's over three hundred years old. I don't know how she came to own it. She must have picked it up in her travels. Nina enjoyed collecting interesting things."

Aunt Emily tapped the key against her other hand. "Thank you, Miss Fields."

"Would you like to visit the theater while you're in town?

Maybe we could meet for dinner?" Miss Fields spoke hesitantly, as if unsure of herself.

"No, thank you," Aunt Emily said. "We appreciate you meeting us here and will certainly be in touch if we have questions."

Miss Fields nodded, then rose and walked to the door. "The front desk knows how to contact me. Enjoy your stay in Portland."

After closing the door behind Miss Fields, Aunt Emily turned back to Eva. "All this way for a mysterious chest? A rather dilapidated one at that. Should we open it now?"

Eva's eyes sparkled. "That's why we came, right?" Sheila had fallen asleep in her arms, so Eva went to make a spot for her to nap on the bed. Once the baby was settled, she hurried back to her aunt.

The chest clearly had a history. Eva wove fanciful images in her head of places and times this chest had seen. She could hardly wait to see what was inside.

Aunt Emily knelt in front of the chest, placed the key into the heart-shaped lock, turned it, and lifted the lid slowly. Stale air carried a scent of decades, of dust and deterioration. Eva leaned forward to get a better look. "I see fabric and paper. Oh, a book!"

Aunt Emily slipped a hand into the chest and retrieved a slim book. "*An Account of My Life's Journey So Far: Its Adversity, Its Sunshine, and Its Clouds.* This is the book Aunt Nina wrote about her life. I'd heard about it but never seen one. She published it herself as a fundraiser for a local charity." She opened the book and paged through it. "This should be interesting. Aunt Nina established the first dancing academy in Portland. She was their most popular teacher, but demanding, too. Practically all of the young men and women of the day attended her classes."

"Our family is so full of accomplished women." Eva reached inside the chest and picked up an oval, cloth-wrapped lump. "Let's empty it first, then pick what to unwrap first." She laid the cloth-wrapped item on the sofa next to her.

"All right," Aunt Emily said. She carefully lifted a stack of newspaper clippings and placed them on the floor. Beneath them was a silk gown. Aunt Emily started to unfold it, but Eva stopped her.

"Empty the whole thing first! We agreed!" Eva laughed as Aunt Emily reluctantly put down the dress.

"All right, you pick one more, then we'll look at them," Aunt Emily said.

Eva nodded and picked up a silk pouch. She put it next to the cloth-wrapped bundle and smiled at Aunt Emily. Then she hurried to remove a handful of other items, placing them on the floor next to the chest before they could tempt her. Reaching into the chest once more, Eva discovered it was empty when she knocked her hand against the bottom of the trunk, creating a hollow thump. She pushed around the edges of the bottom, and it popped up. "Ooooo a false bottom!" Taking out the wooden bottom revealed a cavity. Eva reached in and pulled out a tattered volume. "Another book? This one's handwritten." It had no title, but paging through it quickly revealed it was a journal. Eva frowned. "I wonder how this differs from her published memoir?" She sighed. "I want to read every word, but I want to unwrap all these things, too."

Eva and her aunt turned to the assorted bundles on the floor. Some were flat tissue-wrapped fabric, and others cloth-wrapped lumps. "This one first," Eva said. Carefully unwrapping it, she found a wooden ship model, less than a foot in length. "This is old. Look at the designs." She inspected the detailed carving of rowers, with most of the paddles intact, and the pharaoh figure that sat under a canopy. "Exquisite."

Aunt Emily looked up and nodded. "Must be from the *Innocents Abroad* cruise. Nina was on that trip with Mark Twain, you know."

"*Innocents Abroad*? Wasn't that a book he wrote?"

"Yes. A group of Americans left New York aboard the *Quaker City* for a cruise to the Holy Land. I think it was 1867. They were gone for five months."

Eva scanned the souvenir plates on the wall, trying to match designs to the little ship. "It's maybe Egyptian?"

Aunt Emily picked up Nina's published memoir. "There must be something in here."

Eva rewrapped the ship and picked up the handwritten journal in her lap. "And in here." She paged through the journal until she found the entry.

Cairo, 1867: The desert's oppressive heat crushes us from all sides. I long ago gave up any pretense of comfort. The Great Pyramid towers in the near distance, and the Sphinx glares over our heads. The five in our party separate from the rest of our Great Excursion, who are busy climbing the pyramids.

All the American and European women carry parasols, and everyone wears hats against the fierce sun. In the market near the pyramids, stalls sell figs and oranges, crocodile teeth, scarab jewelry, bits of porcelain, bead necklaces, and pieces scavenged from mummy wrappings. Men and boys display baskets of ghastly merchandise: swathed legs and feet, dried and blackened hands still with red-tinted nails. One of our party, however, wants a complete mummy, and he insists on choosing his own to bring back to the United States. Hence, our journey to the Land of the Dead.

Our guide lights candles for us and disappears through the opening. Mr. Brown follows. I take off my Panama hat and crawl through. The candlelit passage is tall enough for me to stand. I don't bother to brush the dust from my clothing because my eyes widen at the mummies that surround us. The passage is choked with cloth-wrapped bodies, whole and in fragments. Artifacts lie on the floor for the taking, and members of our group pick them up. I am no exception.

I pick up a wooden ship model. The blue and gold paint can still be seen in places not ravaged by time. The figures aboard the ship, the sails and rudder, have been carved by a master. Our guide grins at me and hands me a cloth bag to hold my treasure.

Much later, once more aboard the Quaker City and steaming out of the harbor, I attempt to fit my precious artifact into my suitcase. Alas, we are nearing the end of our journey and my suitcase is simply too full. I have overdone the purchase of artifacts in the Holy Land, so I peruse the pile and select those I can do without in order to make room for my Egyptian ship. I ask a few of my fellow excursionists if they wish to take possession of these artifacts, but everyone has their own stash. There is no room on board at all, so some of the passengers toss the unwanted relics over the rail. Mr. Clemens seems to see only me.

Eva grasped the ship tighter. "A tomb artifact." Holding it brought her closer to an ancestor who had intimately known Mark Twain when he was still Samuel Clemens, and who had thrown priceless artifacts into the sea. Eva wasn't naive. She knew that tourists acquired all sorts of artifacts from places around the world, but it made her skin crawl to learn something that had survived thousands of years had been disposed of in such a careless manner. This action would mar the retelling of the story when she shared it with Sheila. Eva wanted her daughter to admire her ancestors' actions, not be embarrassed by them.

She skipped ahead in the journal to Nina's return and summarized it for Aunt Emily. "It says here that Mark Twain included a bit about Nina disposing of artifacts in one of his dispatches to the California newspaper. The shockwave of public reaction ruined her reputation in New York. Society treated her poorly, and her husband eventually divorced her."

Aunt Emily looked thoughtful. "I didn't know anything about her husband. I do know she never liked Mark Twain."

"Now you know why," Eva said. "He ruined her reputation and cost her a husband. There must have been some issues with him, though, before she left. Otherwise, wouldn't he have accompanied her on the voyage?"

"You're right," Aunt Emily said. "Some distant uncle went with her instead." She found the section in Nina's published memoir that referenced the trip to the Holy Land. "This is brief. It lists some of the passengers and where they stopped. Here it is. On October 2, she mentions Egypt." Aunt Emily frowned. "Nothing about artifacts or tombs or Mark Twain. One thing I've learned about different sides to a story is that the truth is somewhere in the middle."

"You mean Mark Twain wasn't entirely evil and Nina not entirely innocent?" Eve said with a smile. "However it arrived in our family, this artifact deserves reverence." Carefully rewrapping the model ship, she placed it back on the sofa.

Eva admired Nina for having the courage to embark on the cruise to the Holy Land in the first place. She sighed. How lovely to be able to travel across the world and see such inspiring sights, creating such incredible memories. Eva wondered if Nina ever regretted ridding herself of the artifacts she'd collected. At least she'd saved the wooden ship. Eva looked around the room. She saw nothing else that looked like an artifact from the Holy Land.

"Let's see what else we have." Aunt Emily unfolded the silk gown that was full of lace and beads. "This must be from her stage role in New York. It's a bit ostentatious for Portland."

"An actress in the family would have been quite scandalous after the Civil War," Eva said. She gave her aunt a teasing smile, knowing Aunt Emily lived an unconventional life, too.

Now fifty-seven, Aunt Emily had been living with her business partner, Lillian Palmer, for decades. Aunt Emily was an architect who built homes throughout Northern California, while Auntie Lil was a coppersmith who designed beautiful lamps and lighting fixtures. Maybe the women in Eva's life who lived on their own terms fascinated her because of the normality of her own life.

Eva had been married to Teddy for almost two years. So far, Sheila was their only child. She loved them both, she really did, but the reality of being a wife and mother didn't compare to her youthful dreams. Nor did it live up to the legacy of the independent women of her family. Every day, she reminded herself that she was only twenty-two and had a lot of time for adventures, a lot of time to restart the photography business Teddy had made her close. She missed taking photographs like she would miss breathing.

Aunt Emily held up the dress and shook it out. Created of bronze-colored silk, the gown was cut slim in front, with a low neckline and three-quarter length sleeves. Aunt Emily turned the gown to fluff out a voluminous amount of fabric in the back. A piece of paper fell out of the folds.

Eva picked it up. "It's a playbill."

Aunt Emily turned the gown back to the front, which had horizontal stripes of lace, embellished with glass beads and the lacy ruffles along the hem.

Eva peered at the playbill. "In New York, *The Lily of France*, December 1872."

"Let's see what her memoir says." Aunt Emily paged through the book. "Here it is:

> I took lessons in elocution while in New York and traveled the East with an acting troupe, so bad and poorly managed that our performances sometimes drew not a single patron. Then, I got the starring role of Joan of Arc in *The Lily of France* and used the stage name Helen Temple. The show got a lukewarm reaction, but my performance won rave reviews. It was the pinnacle of my career.

"Imagine playing to an empty house, Eva!"

"But starring as Joan of Arc sounds quite grand! Let's see what her journal can tell us," Eva said.

> *New York, 1872: In October, the* New York Herald *talked of my lead role in* Othello. *The paper called me an actress of great ability, possessed of a voice of wonderful sweetness and great power. I have long felt that my life's purpose is to be on the stage. I studied elocution from a fine teacher. I have some knowledge of elocution, gymnastics, and stage business. If my theater career stalls, I hope to have the courage to teach these subjects to other aspiring actresses.*
>
> *By a fortunate circumstance I became acquainted with John Brougham of Wallack's theater, a fine comedian and author of plays, besides. He has written a drama called* Lily of France,

based on Joan of Arc. It is to have an engagement at Booth's Twenty-Third Street theater in November.

The Booth Theater is only a few years old, designed by Edwin Booth, brother of the despicable man who assassinated Papa's friend, President Lincoln. This most modern of theaters is one of the first in New York to have a sprinkler system for fire prevention. The stage deck has double floors, with two spiral staircases at the rear, leading to four fly galleries. It is beautiful and efficient; nonetheless, I am relieved I have no scenes requiring me to fly. Some sort of hydraulic contraption backstage raises bridges and platforms to change the scenery, and the stage lights are electric. They are able to be turned off at once, plunging the theater and stage into complete darkness. I'm sure my heart will stop if that happens while I'm onstage!

So Mr. Bangs graces us with his presence, and my heart is already fluttering at the opportunity to work in this amazing theater. When the actor turns his smile on me, I melt. Something about his curly dark hair, thick mustache, and light eyes emphasizes charm rather than handsome good looks. He kisses my hand, focuses on me for a scant minute, then moves on. For a moment, I am a fan, clutching the kissed hand to my heart and vowing never to wash it. But then the actress surfaces. After all, I am billed to star alongside Mr. Bangs and must behave accordingly.

On opening night, the lights go up, and I blossom onstage. I love the lights, the crowd, and depicting a story to enthrall an audience. Mr. Bangs shows his true colors, though, as he mugs for the audience during the most climactic scenes. He has a habit of moving and speaking slightly slower than the other actors. It draws attention and makes him the center of every scene. I cannot afford to be irked, though, since being billed with him will cause my own star to rise.

After the performance, the magical glow of the theater follows me home to my lonely apartment. Marcus is not there, but that is no longer unusual. My husband, the love of my life, cannot reconcile my growing popularity with his own lack of such. No, here in this most private of documents, I must be honest. After our voyage to the Holy Land, Mr. Clemens' public words destroyed what was left of my marriage.

As actresses do, I peruse every review I can find.

The Era, *a paper in London*, says "Of Miss Ada Ward, who was Cornelia, and Miss Helen Temple, who represented the amorous widow, we can only say that they looked very pretty in very elegant costumes, and there our praise must end."

The New York Herald *is no better.* "The traditional acting of the 'stars' of the sensational drama is not more ridiculous than Miss Temple urging forward her forces on the ramparts of Orleans."

Later, in the same article, I read, "Joan of Arc's contest with Talbot is an episode as ghoulish as it is unworthy of dramatic art."

And finally, "A more thoroughly uncultivated actress never undertook a leading part on the New York stage. Her voice is hollow and without a pleasant tone in its entire range, which sometimes reaches even the boisterous. Her acting is scarcely deserving of the name."

I am shocked and crushed that my performance has stirred such ire among critics. At least one of them acknowledged that with a great deal of study I might improve and become fairly trained. Apparently, despite my elocution lessons, my voice is forceful but weak. Another way of saying nothing while putting down words. The same critic goes on to say that the only bright spot was Mr. George Beck's portrayal of the Court Jester, especially his conversation with his little white dog. Personally, I think the addition of a little white dog detracts from Joan of Arc's story.

I'm a professional, so I ignore the bad reviews and continue to ply my trade. But no one will hire an actress so thoroughly panned. A letter arrives from my elderly mother in California. Since my father's death three years ago, she has grieved. I don't doubt their love, but every time I read her letters, in my mind I see the back of her hand dramatically placed against her forehead as she sighs. In her letter, she orders me home. The reviews of my performance in The Lily of France *have reached California, and she is embarrassed. Better for everyone if her soon-to-be divorced actress daughter returns home where she can be hidden from public view. I know this is her fault for telling all her friends that Miss Helen Temple is, in reality, her own daughter, but I decline to say so. Instead, I comply and become Mrs. Nina Larowe, once again a resident of Nevada City, California.*

"Oh my," Eva murmured. "She came to California after that play closed."

Aunt Emily looked at her with a raised eyebrow. "Yes, that's right. I know she did a few performances in Reno before her mother passed away." She waved her hand in the air. "Then she was in Arizona, New Mexico, all over the place, before ending up here in Portland. Never again in New York, though."

Aunt Emily tucked the playbill back into the chest with the dress. Eva imagined it took strength to continue despite setbacks. Nina had given up her dream of an illustrious acting career, but couldn't resist the limelight.

Eva reached for the silk-wrapped parcel, still looking for the best of Great-Aunt Nina's story. She carefully unrolled it, realizing it was actually a silk bag. Loosening the drawstring, she pulled out a brass spyglass with a handle of carved scrimshaw. Eva peered between the horizontal lines of vines and ropes to read the inscription. "Look ye out to sea for me. From atop the walk ye see topsails come a-home to thee."

"A paramour, perhaps?" Aunt Emily said.

Eva extended the spyglass to its full length and peered through it. "Romantic gift. Maybe from a sea captain? Where would Nina have met a sea captain?" She handed the spyglass to Aunt Emily and read from one of the first pages of the journal.

Valparaiso, 1861: At the age of eighteen, I am ripped from the home I treasure in California. My father, appointed by his friend, President Lincoln, to the post of consul in Valparaiso, Chile, bundles up the family and whisks us off to the mountainous country where we live for the next three years. My brother, Ney, a year younger than I, makes friends easily with native boys and flirts with native girls. It is harder for me, watched closely by Mother. Her first daughter, my stepsister, married two years ago and lives happily in the gold mining town of Red Dog, California, with her husband and toddler daughter. That leaves me as Mother's sole responsibility.

The city of Valparaiso is one street wide in places, but never more than three. It's practically vertical, with steep staircases accessing the houses that cling to the hills, as if by magic, and look serenely out over the harbor, which almost always has an American man-of-war in port. The Jewel of the Pacific, they call this city. It's colorful and noisy and full of European immigrants heading to California. It is also full of enterprising young naval officers visiting my father from the ships.

Our house lies under the big American consulate flag, near the United States Marine Hospital. The house has iron balconies at each window. It is the custom here for young ladies, such as myself, to stand on the balcony and gaze below upon a range of suitors. *The young men in the street look up, much like Romeo in Verona. One of the residents of our house, though, is the big dog, Bosun, who barks at anyone who lingers in front of our house.*

Not long after we arrive, President José Joaquín Pérez Mascayano leaves his home in Santiago, the capital, to visit Valparaiso. Both English-speaking and Chilean residents must fête him properly. Mother and I sew several beautiful gowns, as my father and family are invited to both grand balls. The English ball is magnificent and elegant, but the Chilean ball is brilliant. The dresses are fancier, the jewelry more dazzling, and the dances more graceful.

Father is busy with a group of American naval officers, and as we cannot enter the ball unescorted, an old gray commodore takes my mother's arm, and a young lieutenant takes mine. I've always liked red hair, and the lieutenant's is a rich color and wavy. He is the ne plus ultra *of manly perfection and arouses the utmost admiration. It is possible, as my father later says, that his good looks are embellished by his gorgeous blue uniform with its gold trim. I believe that to be unkind.*

The lieutenant dances with me the requisite number of minuets and waltzes that good breeding allows. To my dismay, I don't learn his name.

The next morning, still in the throes of a red-haired man in my dreams, I push aside the curtains and step out onto the balcony. The sun shines brighter here in Chile than anywhere I have lived, and the colors are more vivid. I am relieved I have taken time to dress and do my hair when I see the lieutenant pause in the street below. Bosun barks, and I shout down to shush him.

"I have something for you," the lieutenant calls up to me. He holds up a silk bag to show me, then ties it to Bosun's collar.

"Bosun, come!" I call, using my firm no-nonsense voice.

"Come get a cookie!" If my firm voice doesn't work, the offer of a cookie always does. Loud thumps on the stairway announce the big dog's approach. I snatch a biscuit off my morning tray and give it to Bosun. He munches it as I untie the bag.

Inside is a beautiful brass spyglass, small enough to tuck into a pocket. Its scrimshaw handle is engraved with a message to a sweetheart to watch for her sailor. The lieutenant's forwardness causes me to blush. He is waiting below for my reaction, and I quickly fan myself to cool the heat from my cheeks. I want to be his sweetheart, but what will Mama say? What will Papa say? Returning to the balcony, I hold the spyglass aloft. "It's very pretty, Lieutenant."

He has the grace to look flustered. "It's something my sea captain father gave to my mother. When she passed away, he gave it to me to pass on to a pretty girl. So it is yours." He bows to punctuate his words.

He thinks I'm pretty. I don't know what to say, having no experience with this sort of interaction. He smiles, and my heart flips in my chest.

"Use it to watch for my ship," he says. "I will visit you whenever I am in town."

Before I can do more than smile and nod back, he strides toward the harbor. I tuck the spyglass back into its bag and slip it into my pocket.

About a month passes before the lieutenant's ship returns to Valparaiso, and every month after that, on an almost-regular schedule. I become very good at guessing when to start watching for his ship, and I'm ready for his arrival every time.

Spanish custom dictates that women promenade in the square in front of the cathedral in pairs, followed by their mothers. Men, also in pairs, promenade the opposite way and exchange glances with the women. They are not allowed to speak.

The lieutenant and I become adept at exchanging glances. I flutter my eyelashes and keep my head down, picturing the brown lashes sweeping my milky cheek. In my mind's eye, I see him grasp my hand in a burst of wickedness. He never does.

When the captain visits my father, the lieutenant accompanies him. The men sit in the parlor with Mother and I. Father talks to the captain, and Mother watches closely as the lieutenant and I discuss the weather and other mundane topics. We are never able to speak privately, and I fear my longings will burst from me and embarrass us all.

Mother tells me it is proper for a man to propose to the mother on behalf of her daughter if he is serious about a relationship. Then, an engagement is worked out between the man and the parents without so much as a word to the bride-to-be. It dismays me that the lieutenant is not interested in pursuing me to that end, but how would he know if I am the one he wishes to marry? He's never spoken to me of my wishes for the future or desires for a family, and no happy marriage is based on conversations about clouds and rain.

Six months before we leave our post in Valparaiso, the lieutenant stops coming. I never stop using the spyglass to watch for him, and I never learn his name.

"Romantic but sad," Aunt Emily said as she handed the spyglass back to her niece.

Eva placed the spyglass back into its silk bag, sad that it wasn't set out on display in Nina's apartment. But if Nina had been able to stay in Chile with her lieutenant, or sail away with him, she never would have gone on the voyage with Mark Twain or tried to become an actress. Would she have been happier?

Looking back on choices that could have been made,

however, never solved anything. It was like Eva asking herself if she should have kept her photography business in Inverness, California. Teddy had insisted her role as wife and mother would take up too much time for a business. Eva had agreed because she loved him. She still did. But she loved photography, too, even if these days, it was limited to pictures of family.

Sheila's cries broke her reverie. "Be right back," she told her aunt. She put the rewrapped spyglass on the couch next to the wooden ship and stood up to go to her daughter.

In the bedroom, Eva picked up the baby and bounced her lightly in her arms until the baby fell back to sleep. Since her daughter's birth, Eva had been extremely conscious of legacy. She would tell Sheila the stories of her ancestors, and she'd be there to encourage her daughter to pursue whatever path she desired. What if Sheila struggled? Or chose an inappropriate path? Eva shook her head. Sheila would inevitably have disappointments in her life. It was beyond Eva's imagination, though, to look at her sweet baby's face and see disappointment or despair.

Returning to the front room, Eva sat on the couch and arranged Sheila in her lap. Aunt Emily was reading a page in Nina's memoir. "Here it says the family arrived in Nevada from Chile in 1863, but without James. He apparently sent his wife home from Valparaiso with the children, while he went off to Bolivia in search of gold." She turned the page. "Nina met Samuel Clemens in Virginia City about this time. And she married Marcus Larowe there in 1864." She looked up at Eva. "That's not much of a courtship. I wonder if she knew him in California before they left for Chile?"

"No," Eva said. "She must have met Marcus after she arrived in Nevada. Just imagine, she might have married Mark Twain instead! Maybe they would have gotten along better on the cruise four years later." She laughed and Aunt Emily joined in.

Nothing Nina attempted had truly given her the esteem she craved. Eva stood up as Aunt Emily repacked the chest. Taking Sheila on a tour of the room, she inspected her great aunt's apartment with new eyes. Everything was placed just so, as if on display for visitors. How many society visitors had Nina truly entertained? Her memoir seemed to have been written by a society maven while her journal was penned by a woman dogged by disappointments. Eva kissed the top of Sheila's head and murmured sweet nothings into her ear.

Aunt Emily picked up the stack of newspaper clippings and said, "Look, these are all from the last years of Nina's life." She riffled through the clippings. "Most of these are announcements of dance parties and recitals. She did some dramatic readings and one-woman performances." She read a few more pieces, then said, "Oh, listen to this. She's talking about the Turkey Trot dance. 'It's like a turkey on a hot plate, constantly lifting its feet so they won't get burned. When danced in the extreme, heads are held very close together—too close together, I should say.' I wonder what she had to say about other dances, like the Grizzly Bear or Texas Tommy? The Bunny Hug probably made her apoplectic!" Aunt Emily laughed.

Eva sat down on the couch. Before this trip, her interest in Nina had stemmed from her curiosity about how much Great Aunt Nina's lifestyle had embarrassed and angered her mother. On this trip, Eva learned about a woman who had been to amazing places in her lifetime and done amazing things. Even more important, though, were the journal's revelations. Nina had setbacks along the way but never let them control her. She'd shown bravery and persistence.

Eva felt greater empathy for Nina now that she knew more

about her life and her emotions. Maybe that's what she needed to communicate in the stories she'd tell Sheila about her ancestors, that there was more to a person than their actions and accomplishments. She'd show her daughter how to feel empathy, as well as pride, for women who came before her. She would nurture in Sheila the traits that made the women in her family strong. As for herself, she would work every day to be a great wife and mother, and someday, she'd reopen her photography business. It was a goal to inspire her, a life worth living, a legacy to be proud of.

The next day, the bellman removed Nina's chest along with their luggage as the women began their journey home to California. Aunt Emily admonished him to handle the chest carefully. Eva, with Sheila in her arms, held her head high and walked through the opulent lobby of the Multnomah Hotel. Great Aunt Nina had pushed forward, never resting on her laurels or bemoaning her losses. She persevered in reinventing herself as she needed to, with grace and confidence in public and honesty in the privacy of her journal. She'd taken her place among the best of Portland society with her room in the best hotel in the Northwest. Eva wondered how many other fascinating stories lay behind the Mulnomah's grandeur and was glad she'd discovered Nina's.

"The beauty of family history is in knowing more than the stories," Eva said to her daughter. "Nina Larowe might not have been legendary, but through her persistence she enjoyed success. Someday, sweetheart, I will tell you all about her, and about Aunt Emily's creativity and my own empathy. You will be proud of your true legacy."

Linda Ulleseit believes in the unspoken power of women living ordinary lives. Her book, and the story "True Legacy" are the stories of women in her family who were extraordinary but unsung. For more about Eva Walters and Emily Williams, read *Under the Almond Trees*. For more about Nina Larowe's parents and family, read *The River Remembers*, coming June 2023 from She Writes Press. For more of Nina Larowe's story, follow Linda as she writes *Innocents At Home*. Visit her website at ulleseit.com and follow her on Facebook, Bookbub and Instagram.

For more about Eva Walters and Emily Williams, read Under the Almond Trees. *For more about Nina Larowe's parents and family, read* The River Remembers, *coming June 2023 from She Writes Press. For more of Nina Larowe's story, follow Linda on social media as she writes* Innocents At Home.

THREADBARE LINENS
BY MARI ANNE CHRISTIE

CHARLESTON, SOUTH CAROLINA, SEPTEMBER, 1862

Ruthie Telfair gently laid her great-grandmother's table linens across the top of the day-to-day house linens. She closed and locked the old chest she had been gifted by her noble relations during the Grand Tour of the Continent she'd taken with her husband for their tenth anniversary, which was antique long before she took possession. Strong, heavy, sturdy wood, with two worn-down family crests on the sides and a heart-shaped carving around a broken lock. If she had to guess, she'd say it was centuries old, weathered, certainly, but in remarkably good shape, as though it had been restored. Aside from her linens, indisputably women's work, the chest contained a false bottom, beneath which Ruthie kept correspondence she didn't wish her father to find and any monies her endlessly wealthy brother, Harry Wentworth, found a way to surreptitiously contribute to the household—against their father's long-standing ban on his support.

Currently, the secret compartment held, in addition to a goodly portion of the money he'd sent since the war started, many thousands in gold and Confederate dollars her brother had foisted upon her not a month ago, when she traversed enemy waters to find him at Riverwood Plantation. He'd been holed up there for months, living in Union-occupied territory on a Charleston barrier island. The land was rightly owned by the Guignard family, who'd fled just ahead of the first Union forces. Ruthie could hardly credit Harry's stupidity, for such a brilliant newspaperman. Writing editorials denouncing the South from a short boat ride away was naught but suicide, no matter how many enemy soldiers he had in his pocket.

Ruthie wished she had the time to press the tablecloths and serviettes. Or, to be honest, she wished she had the servants to do it in her stead, while she focused her attention on her children and benevolent works in her community. She wished she could spend the money in her keeping without it being known where it came from, branding her a traitor in her own house, to say nothing of the world outside. She wished the North had left well enough alone and her life had never changed. But instead, she was the keeper of everyone's secrets, foremost, her brother Harry's.

She used to have three closets filled with linens in the city house; six at the plantation, and now, after donating the vast majority of her sheets and towels to the Confederate hospital, she was reduced to this chest. Enough for one extra change of bed linen for each of them and her great-grandmother's table linens. And only one servant who could be compelled to press them but was more useful elsewhere.

Servants. Her brother, the great Harry Wentworth, ever the populist, would say she should call them slaves for the sake of accuracy, but she'd been taught all her life the word was vulgar, and nothing was more sinful in Charleston Society than vulgarity, especially of the honest variety. Besides, just see where that kind of hostility had gotten Harry—Father actively homicidal and his friends egging him on to do who knows what to his son. She'd been reduced to listening at keyholes with her mother, in the hopes they could head off any acts of aggression before they began.

No need to listen at keyholes now, she thought, the way her father was bellowing. She wished he would take her mother's delicate health into consideration when he began to shout. The news of her condition had only fed his anger; he blamed Harry entirely for breaking his mother's heart.

"I'll not have it! I'll not have that blasphemous traitor spouting his treason all over the world from a stone's throw away. No, he should have stayed in the North where he belongs, and I am just the man to send him there!"

Her mother's voice was muted; Ruthie strained to hear her. She only knew whatever she said would be soothing and would play on what tiny bit of familial empathy any father might feel for any son. Mother would never outright contradict him, but she would kindly point out that Harry was their only son, no matter how many times he was disowned, and she refused to stop acknowledging that she loved him. Such was her faith that her husband, Second Wentworth, would never raise a hand to a woman, especially a woman under his protection. Ruthie wasn't so sure.

Even so, she was not at all soothing when her father started one of his rants against her brother. The last time she had stood up for Harry, her father threatened to put her out of the house if she ever again used money from Harry toward their support. Ruthie was fairly certain that was the last time he would allow. Now, she wasn't to spend any money he hadn't handed her himself, no matter how little that might be. She didn't speak until she was spoken to, either, most often engaged by her mother making an obvious change of subject—the weather or a call they'd paid. It was their job, as ladies of the house, to maintain decorum in the face of this everlasting war in her family and her homeland.

"Miz Ruthie," Elias whispered.

Elias had been Harry's best childhood friend, his milk brother, and companion to both Wentworth children. And he had been Second Wentworth's possession nearly all his life. He was among the longest-lasting, best links she had to her brother, even down to the present day, carrying messages to him in hostile territory, under her father's nose.

"Miz Ruthie, Mama told me to tell you some things."

Yes, now would be an excellent time to pass information without her father hearing it—no one in earshot of him could hear a thing—and anything Nancy, Elias's mama and Ruthie's childhood Nonny, had to say was worth attention. Her mother would want to hear it, too, but that could wait. Ruthie closed the trunk and motioned for Elias to join her just inside the door to the dusty music room, which had once been the site of celebrated musicales.

"She heard Mister Wentworth talking to Mister Whaley and two other Misters while you and Miz Emily were out at the Ansons. They make their plans for tonight; eight men going to Riverwood after dark. Three boats."

Ruthie's stomach fell. She'd known it was coming for weeks now, and she was lucky to have a few hours' warning, but it didn't make it any less horrifying to know her father would likely attempt to kill his son and had rallied seven other men with him. She hoped her sons weren't involved, but she was afraid they were. They were almost old enough for military service now, and thought themselves even older. They only remained home from the fighting because she encouraged them to believe their mother needed their protection. And perhaps she did.

"What are they planning? Did she hear?"

"Nothing else, just tonight after dark, eight men, three boats."

"That's it, then. It's time."

"I think it is, Miz Ruthie. Mama packing a bag for me right now. Will take a lot of luck to get there in time."

Ruthie could only imagine, after her own foray across the river, through two armies, to Riverwood Plantation in Harry's old skiff, not a month past. She only hoped Elias was better prepared than she had been and had as much sheer luck. At least he was wearing the same coat; the one Harry had commissioned for him decades ago, with enough hiding places sewn in to move hundreds of thousands of dollars or more in currency, gold, gems, and financial paperwork. Ruthie had an idea what Elias might have hidden in his coat, having traversed the river wearing it filled with banknotes and gold and rough gemstones a few weeks ago that were now hidden in the linen chest. She resolved not to ask him what he was taking with him. Who knew how much of Harry's money Elias had saved? Whatever it was, he'd more than earned it in almost sixty years serving in her father's house.

"My mother has the paperwork for you."

Ruthie's mother had promised Elias his freedom, if he would voluntarily participate in her plan to keep her son safe from his father. Ruthie was fairly certain he would have done it without the incentive, but more was at stake than one man's freedom. Harry had asked Ruthie to watch the next slave auction for his people, should they be captured and sold, which was likely if his avaricious—destitute—father confiscated them. "Send Jeremiah to Harry's man of business and tell him the gold will be waiting as arranged."

"Will do that, Miz Ruthie, but tonight I'll do whatever I can for Mister Harry. His people have to fend for themselves until we can get to them. If Mister Wentworth doesn't just kill them outright."

At the look on Ruthie's face, Elias said, more gently than she deserved, "All due respect, Miz Ruthie, all of us knew the risks better than you did. Every one of us knows we might die for Mister Harry someday. Just happens might be tonight." He paused and reached out a hand to touch her elbow, something he'd never in their lives done, even at the cost of letting her stumble. "I expect this might be the last time we see each other."

And probably the last time he would ever see his mother, Ruthie surmised, but didn't say. Unspoken was the hope that Ruthie would be benevolent and take care of her Nonny, to say nothing of her own mother, her father and sons, her maid and the boy, Jeremiah, and now five darkies Harry had placed under her dubious protection in a ridiculous plan. As much as she wanted to reassure Elias when he was off to be of aid to her brother, she couldn't bring herself to make one more promise she mightn't be able to keep. She would do her best by Nonny. She could only do her best.

"I am glad you will be free, all these years you've been at my father's whim. You deserve this. Harry is right."

Elias was giving up everything for his loyalty to Harry, and for his freedom. Ruthie wasn't quite sure yet how loyal she could afford to be to Harry, but after the way his money had kept them all afloat these past months, and would going forward, she would fulfill as many of his requests as she could without endangering herself.

Her father slammed a door and said, at volume: "I'm going to the Club. Don't expect me for supper," and her mother slipped out of the parlor when he stomped out the front door. Ruthie caught her eye and motioned to the music room.

"It's time," was all her mother said. Ruthie nodded and Elias twisted his hat in his hands.

"Elias, I have your papers in my writing desk, with a pass." They all filed down the hall to the parlor, where Father had been making his displeasure known only minutes before. Ruthie could still feel his hatred for Harry lingering in the air.

As she crossed to the desk to remove the manumission papers and the nighttime pass, Emily said: "They aren't truly legal without my husband's signature, but they will bear up under most scrutiny. If Mister Wentworth catches you..."

"That's true no matter how I go or when," Elias said.

"Keep the manumission papers well-hidden until you get to the Union Army," Emily advised, though Ruthie would daresay Elias, as he said, knew the risks better than they did. "Keep the pass at hand in the city. I shall sign them in my husband's name and send you on your way. I hope you can make it to Riverwood before my husband convenes his posse; I think they will wait until full dark to go."

Emily would never tell Elias not to put himself in danger. To her mind, the manumission papers she had signed were payment for putting himself in danger. Ruthie, though, knew Harry would wish Elias safe. Harry would rather be at risk himself than see his oldest friend in jeopardy. Ruthie would rather neither of them be a target this night, but she wasn't a foolish woman.

"Ruthie, can you make certain the kitchen prepares some food for Elias to take with him?"

"Mama took care of that," Elias told Emily, "and packed a bag waiting in the kitchen. Miz Emily, Miz Ruthie, I want to thank you for my freedom," he gestured with the papers he was folding to insert into the hem of his coat, "and for trusting me to warn Mister Harry. For taking care of me and my mama all these years when Mister Wentworth would have sold us off. You been kind to us."

"You've been more than loyal, Elias; you and Nancy both," Emily said. Ruthie followed with, "You have both meant so much to our families. You mean so much to Harry."

"If I'm gon' get to him, I have to go."

"Godspeed, Elias," Emily said as Ruthie raised her hand to wave goodbye to Elias's back, headed toward the kitchen. When she stepped forward as though to follow, Emily said, "No, let him speak to Nancy alone. It may be the last time."

Ruthie stepped back, at a loss as to what to do next.

"Now," her mother said, "we must make ourselves ready for any eventuality, and we must wait. I suggest we take up our needlework." Needlework was code for mending. There was no time for embroidery when there was a household of five to run, with two of them growing boys, and only so many hours of daylight.

Not a quarter-hour later, Ruthie looked up when her mother slumped suddenly, mid-sentence, over the collar she was turning. She threw down the chemise she was working on and rushed across the room. But she was too late. Before Ruthie could even bend over the chair, Emily was dead.

Five days later, her mother had been buried, and Ruthie still hadn't heard a word about her brother, not even from her father, who was usually prone to braggadocio. That night, the one that changed everything, her father had come home as per his usual, around nine o'clock, to the news that his wife was dead, his groom had escaped his ownership, his daughter was distraught, and his household was in general chaos. Ruthie took only enough time from her grief that night to note her father was wearing different clothes when he came home.

Ruthie doubted Harry was dead, for surely his body would have turned up by now, and it would be front-page news in every major city on the planet. But there were many fates worse than death Ruthie could imagine, endless forms of torture and countless ways a body could disappear. She had no way of knowing what her father and his friends had done unless someone told her, which could not happen because she was stuck inside with her family in mourning.

After an initial show of community support, the family was expected to withdraw from Society for a time. Her father's rants now turned to Elias using his wife's death to escape enslavement. Her father assumed Elias had sought the Union Army, using all that occurred that night as a distraction. He hadn't a notion Elias would dare to defy him so thoroughly as to try to warn Harry.

Ruthie went on arranging for the household to run as smoothly as could be expected with only one maid plus a nursemaid turned cook and a boy of all work. Father continued to spend most of his time at his club—had begun taking her boys there with him—and did not make any special effort to communicate with Ruthie about anything. She had crossed too many lines defending Harry, clearly. And her father was grieving his wife in the manner any angry man would.

Ruthie didn't change into mourning black because she was already wearing it, after the deaths of so many of her relatives and friends. Her one black dress had been her day dress since it became clear she would have to take on household chores. The black hid the dirt as well as anything, but it was only one more reminder of all she had lost the past two years.

It wasn't that she didn't grieve Emily's sudden death; only that she had too many losses and too many worries to grieve her mother properly. Not least, she was left alone with her father—who might literally be willing to kill her—and her sons, who were almost like strangers these days.

Jeremiah was waiting for her when she went out into the yard. "Miz Ruthie?" He looked around. "I got news," he said at a whisper, holding out a note. She went to him and took the missive; it could be anything, from any of a dozen people, any of whose contact might see her father kill her.

She sent up a prayer that it was news of Harry.

"Ma'am, there is gossip saying a conjure woman been working with a Union Army doctor at Port Royal to save 'the newspaperman'." There was only one newspaperman in the vicinity important enough to be known as such. "He's in a bad way, Miz Ruthie, but he's alive and Elias is with him. That's all I heard at the Market, but it's something."

Ruthie breathed in suddenly, a bit lightheaded at this bittersweet news. If only she knew from what he needed saving. If only they were farther away from Harry's father. Port Royal wasn't nearly far enough, no matter how many Yankee soldiers stood between Second Wentworth and his son.

"Let me read this."

As it happened, the note was from Harry's one South Carolina man of business—

Purchase complete. Transport arranged to countryside. God help them.

Ruthie let go a deep breath.

Mr. Clarkson lived far outside the confines of Charleston Society; he was the first stop on any route Harry established to get out of town. He had been one of Harry's Charleston men of business, until Harry was ostracized and left with only the one. He had posed as a Cuban landowner at the first slave auction after the incident, buying up Harry's "servants who were not slaves," and probably more. He likely knew less than Ruthie of the attack—he had only been carrying out orders Harry left with them, to be set in motion in the event of emergency—but he certainly knew more about whatever it was Harry did with the slaves and former slaves he and his friends spirited out of Charleston.

Harry's man of business had arranged the purchase, outfitted, and then transported all the slaves he'd purchased to Ruthie's husband's country home, Teller Road. From her plantation, Harry's servants could run anywhere they wanted. She had done what she could. She couldn't transport them out of the state, for she had no means to do so, and she had no idea where any Abolitionists might take in runaways. But no one would look for them at Teller Road, and they would have a bit of time to regroup.

She could find one of Harry's land or sea couriers, that Dirk Devlin or Captain Amos Rink. Ruthie did expect them soon, maybe Devlin, maybe Rink, maybe both. They would make contact when they found Harry's home empty; she'd half-expected the news about Harry to come from one of them. She wished she had the wherewithal and freedom to go to Riverwood herself, but Harry himself would tell her not to put herself in that sort of danger when there were professionals in place to manage the details. Ruthie had only to do her part—make sure enough money made it to Harry's man of business.

I could let myself be rescued, she thought briefly, *next dark moon.* She knew the cove where Rink tied up his boat. But given the state of things, she couldn't know for sure Harry's blockade runner would make landfall at the dark moon, or if she could get the skiff to the cove undetected, or when or where or how one of those men might otherwise come calling. Them with their bags of coin and news of Harry and perpetual offers to arrange her transport North with anyone else who could be trusted. In the North, she would live as she always had before the war, under Harry's protection instead of her father's or husband's, with access to Harry's money. *I could let myself be rescued.*

But no, she couldn't leave her boys, especially not with their grandfather. They were now both bigger than she, and there was no chance they would come willingly to Northern territory. Soon they would go to war, and she would have to wait for them to come home. Come what may, she had thrown her lot in with the South and a Southerner she would remain. Besides, there was no telling now whether Harry would even be in a position to protect her.

"Thank you, Jeremiah. I can't give you a wage like my brother does, but you have my thanks." In truth, she could, and would, from Harry's money, if she knew her father wouldn't catch wind of it.

"Mister Harry is good for it, Miz Ruthie." He winked at her, and she started. She'd never been so informal with her servants as to have them touching her arm or winking at her.

Ruthie felt like celebrating her brother's survival, if only for a moment. She felt like taking the fine china and silver out of hiding in the root cellar; she would use her great-grandmother's table linens from the linen chest, press them herself. This news warranted rejoicing, in a manner her father could hardly question, as often as he decried the informality of modern life in a war zone. Her brother and Elias were alive and with the Union Army. She had fulfilled her promise to Harry and saved at least five black souls from her father's wrath. And it was time to get supper started.

Two hours later, when they sat down to supper on the good china and her great-grandmother's table linens, the first thing Second said from his seat at the head of the table was, "I came into some money today." It had been a long time since he had said such a thing; before the war, when there was always plenty, he never discussed money, and after secession, when he "invested" nearly every penny they had in the Confederacy, there was none to speak of.

Perhaps it would be enough to supplement the hominy and yams they were eating, the last of their stores. She only wasted a moment recalling the plethora of dishes straining her brother's table a month ago, setting her mouth watering. Fried chicken, ham, snap beans with bacon, cornbread with butter and blackberry jam… coffee… no, it did no good to think of it. She wished Harry's messengers would bring her foodstuffs she could tell her father she'd acquired through barter, instead of more infernal money she couldn't use.

He handed her 100 Confederate dollars, most likely his cut of whatever the eight men had collectively been paid for Harry's servants, less the price of his bill at the Charleston Club. Her heart sank. She knew Harry's agent had paid in gold; Harry never did business any other way. Her father had, once again, bought useless Confederate paper with any gold he came across. The notes were worth half the value they held a year ago–barely more than the paper they were printed on–and if Harry had impressed nothing else on her, it was how much worse that would be shortly. At least she had the money in hiding to make up the difference between what her father thought a Confederate dollar would buy, and what it actually could.

She made appropriate noises of gratitude for the nothing Second had provided to keep his family, and hastened the dinner conversation along, hoping in vain to get through the entire meal without discussion of all the ways Harry had betrayed the South or the places Elias might be hiding. He was beginning to sound more than eccentric, with only two topics of conversation. He sounded a bit unhinged.

Shortly after supper, her father and her sons repaired to their club, presumably to relive the horror of whatever they had done to her brother. Her heart raced and face flushed as she mended a tear in a bedsheet. She was livid when she thought of how her father had reeled them in. It was reprehensible how he made them into foolish, hate-spouting, uncle-harming reprobates, all by sharing drinks, and probably loose women, which they could all ill afford. She stabbed her needle into the bedsheet. The linens would be threadbare in no time.

Not ten minutes later, Jeremiah slipped into the room.

"Miz Ruthie, a man to see you in the yard." She put aside her mending. Only one type of man showed up in the yard between the house and the stables, directly after all the men in the house had left.

"Is it Mister Devlin or Captain Rink?"

"Mister Devlin, Ma'am."

Here would be real news of Harry. Dirk Devlin would know

anything there was to know, and he would probably have more money she couldn't use.

Dirk bobbed his head and touched his hat brim when she swept into the yard. "Missus Telfair, it is good to see you well. I won't keep you long."

"No, you'd better not. What can you tell me?" She couldn't believe it had been five days and she still didn't know what her father—and probably her sons—had done.

"It's dire, Missus Telfair." He reached into his coat pocket and held out an envelope. "He left this for you at Riverwood in case of emergency, and safe to say, even Harry would agree, we're having an emergency."

"Aren't we just?" She took it and unfolded the letter within, only one page. But still, another thing she would have to hide from her father in the linen chest. She could hardly burn her brother's last words to her.

Ruthie:

Of course, I have left a letter in case of my death or incapacitation, and I am prematurely dismayed at the thought you are reading it now. You may rest assured I am most likely terribly sorry for whatever it is that I did (or didn't do) to warrant whatever may (or may not) happen to me that will result in you reading this. I hope you will keep to the plan as we've defined it— only to the extent you can do so safely—and not let grief or anger toward me color your actions, no matter how much of an ass I might make of myself in what context, especially if it has led to my own suffering. I know that is a sin for which you might never forgive me.

My dearest sister, I should take a moment to express what an honor and privilege it has been to be your brother in this lifetime.

I am not certain I would have survived our father without you, nor become half the man of consequence I am today, if not for you pushing me to envision a larger life for myself than you, as the girl-child, would ever be allowed.

You have constantly astonished me since childhood, with your wit and your sharp, creative mind. Your ability and willingness to debate me on just about anything is at least half responsible for my skill at argumentation. (At which, I must admit, you are more skilled than I. If not for the lottery that made you a woman, and the marriage and family implied therein, it would be you with the global accolades, not I.)

It has been a stone at my heel all these years that our correspondence has been limited by time and [oft but not only geographic] circumstance. And ah, well, now it is likely too late to correct the deficit. I have been a haphazard correspondent with those I love, and I find I regret it now, with one foot into my dotage.

If I am dead by now, I have, of course, remembered you in my will, so do not put off any meetings with my attorneys. I've made all sorts of arrangements for you behind your back, and now you can do nothing but bear the brunt of my love and largesse. I am sincerely sorry for any grief I have caused you, now or in the past (indeed, given the likelihood of posthumous meddling, into the future).

As our grandfather Beaufain once charged me: I hope you will use your inheritance from me to continue your lifetime of honor, dignity, and conscience. I cannot think of anyone I would trust more to live a life in accordance with moral principles.

It was never my intent to hurt anyone; I suspect, in the end, I will have hurt everyone instead.

Yours,
Harry Wentworth

"Tell me, Mr. Devlin... can you tell me the nature of his injuries?"

Dirk winced. "I thought you would know by now. He's in a bad way, Ma'am. Burns, broken bones, near-drowning. He lost two fingers. They took him within inches of his life."

"I knew they would do..." Ruthie's hand shot up to cover her mouth to stop incipient retching. "But it is difficult to hear aloud. Pray, continue."

"The doc is keeping him drugged up pretty heavy to keep him quiet. We don't expect him to wake from the morphine for some time yet. If he does at all."

She didn't realize she'd swayed until his hand reached out to steady her. She could never have imagined such horrific torture meted out by her father against his son. She couldn't believe the legendary voice of the great P.H. Wentworth would be silenced by such a vicious filicide. No, she could not believe it; he would live.

"He's still near Port Royal with Elias, but we will take them both to New York in the next few days."

He was yet breathing, Ruthie thought. He would go to New York where there were no shortages of anything and he would recuperate from the enormous betrayal that was designed to kill him but wouldn't. Couldn't.

"Harry and New York are why I'm here now," Dirk continued. "If he were in any state for it, he'd tell me to grab you up and bring you with us kicking and screaming. No offense meant, Ma'am—only wishing to keep your safety in mind—and we can take up to three other people, too." He paused. "Either race. Any station. As long as they can be trusted."

"No offense taken. I am used to Harry's meddling. His servants are at Teller Road. You should take them with you. Or put them in touch with whoever Harry works with to send slaves North."

"That's in my sights, Missus Telfair, but right now, all due respect, we are doing everything in our power to save Harry. Everyone else has to wait."

Well, if that didn't ever sound like an excuse, Ruthie thought, to leave five unfortunate souls to whatever fate might befall them. But still, she didn't want anyone's attention to turn from her brother's care. Elias and Mr. Devlin were right; Harry's people would have to fend for themselves for a time. She'd done the best she could.

"If you see them, you can tell them Rink's deliveries will be interrupted; it won't work to find the cove at the dark moon anymore. This is your last chance for a good, long while to get out of here, Mrs. Telfair. We'll be back here, I'm sure. I just don't know when, and I'd hate for you to regret anything later."

"I hate to disappoint you and Harry, but once again, I shan't go North with you. I don't suppose it will do any good to send news to him through you now, will it? I needn't pen a note."

"I wouldn't think so, no, Missus Telfair, but if you need him to know anything, I'm happy to keep your confidence in case he comes back to us."

The enormity of what she needed to tell Harry fell like bricks on her shoulders, their mother's death foremost.

"No, there's nothing I can tell him now that will make a bit of difference to his survival, and that must be all that he thinks about, not me and Charleston. If he asks after me, please tell him I love him."

"I will do that, Ma'am. Now, as I say, not sure when I will be back here, so I hope this will tide you over." He took out the ubiquitous sack of gold and silver coin Harry always sent with his courier, considerably larger this time than last. "I'm leaving you all the cash left at Riverwood. Harry's orders."

Of course, they were Harry's orders. More and more and more money always appeared until one couldn't help but do anything he wanted. He'd been doing it ever since he came into his trust at fourteen and started giving the children on the plantation a shinplaster now and again.

"What's more, Ma'am, I've left the last of his food in the lean-to at the docks. You know the one?"

"Of course. And Jeremiah knows it." This was a boon of the sort she could never repay.

"It's not inconsiderable. Rink just brought supplies from New York through the blockade. I suggest you be careful transporting it and don't feed all your hungry neighbors. Harry's instructions said you would know who gets a piece of whatever might spoil, but you should keep a good portion for you and yours."

What a weight from her shoulders—for as long as Harry's food lasted. But replaced with different worries. It's not that she wasn't grateful, but there was always some dangerous part Ruthie had to play, or ask someone else to play, most often defying her father. And Harry always made Ruthie into some sort of Lady Bountiful among the servants. He couldn't stop manipulating everyone around him with money if he wanted to, which he wouldn't ever.

But she could still hear his grave voice lecturing her during her trip to Riverwood, as he packed gems into the seams of the greatcoat. "You cannot imagine how much money it will require to survive what's coming, Ruthie. The paper will go first, then the coin, faster than you can conceive." And wasn't she grateful he wouldn't leave her to starve like so many people would before this war was over?

"I can't imagine we won't see each other again one day, Missus Telfair," Dirk said. "Maybe even soon. But for now, I should go before anyone asks any questions."

"You should. Mr. Devlin, I wish to offer you my thanks for all the many times you have done this, or something like this, meeting with Jeremiah, delivering things to everyone. It's a tremendous risk, and I have never said thank you."

Dirk Devlin's grin seemed as wide as the horizon. "That's what Harry pays me for, Ma'am." With that, he tipped his hat and slipped out of the yard and away from the house.

She wasn't sure so much more money would fit under the false bottom in the linen chest; she might need to hide it in the mending pile. Doling it out, nickel by dime, purely to keep her father from knowing she had it, meant it would probably last forever. Even if her father weren't controlling their finances, she could hardly rub her friends' and neighbors' noses in a sudden windfall, when most of them were suffering lack and deprivation. No, the money would stay well hidden, but for the loose change that could discreetly hold a household together.

For now, she took the time alone in the house to hide this new influx. Harry did always say not to keep all your valuables in one place. A quarter of the cash, by sheer volume, was tucked under the mending pile, half beneath the loose boards in the empty carriage house, and the last quarter with Harry's letter under the chest's false bottom, hidden by the sheets and towels and their great-grandmother's table linens.

Tomorrow, she would take the time to sew part of her new-found fortune into the seams of a gown, the boning of a corset, and the lining of a coat, like the caped greatcoat Elias had taken with him. She should have done it before now. As Harry would surely say, a person never knew when she might need to start anew with nothing but the clothes on her back. It was wartime, after all; anything could happen.

Mari Anne Christie writes second chances for scarred souls. Her literary historical novel, *Blind Tribute*, follows the American Civil War through the eyes of Harry Wentworth, an intrepid journalist with controversial views. In Christie's Unlocked short vignette, "Threadbare Linens," Harry's sister, Ruthie, fights her own war in his absence, keeping Harry's dangerous secrets and her own. For more about Mari, check out her website at www.MariAnneChristie.com, or follow her on Facebook, Twitter, Goodreads, or Bookbub.

A RAREFIED GIFT
BY EDIE CAY

LONDON, ENGLAND, 1823

"You want me to find a wooden box?" Jack Townsend asked, squinting at her. "That may or may not be in London?"

Mina hung her head. She knew it was a Herculean endeavor, and hardly worth the time of someone so well known. But her brother insisted she call on Jack Townsend at his home in Marylebone to ask after the object.

"A wooden box with a heart-shaped lock," Mina said, wringing her handkerchief to naught more than a crumple of threads. Benjamin thought the box might yield information about the family, some relations they might rely on to help with Mina's opportunities. But Mina knew—they were twins after all—that Benjamin was worried about money and couldn't afford to keep up the household for them and their maid-of-all-work, Penny. She knew he didn't want to live separately from her, but money was money.

Jack Townsend's dark eyes suddenly took on a glimmer. A glimmer of hope was the only thing Mina could possibly hope for herself.

"And was there a key to this heart-shaped lock? Dimensions of the box?" Townsend was on his feet in a moment, skirts swishing as he paced.

Mina took a moment to stare at those swishing skirts. Townsend wore a man's waistcoat and cravat—even a fob with a watch. But from behind the desk, Mina hadn't seen the skirts. The skirts? It was not her place to ask questions; it was her place to ask for help. Though it had occurred to her that not asking questions had landed her and Benjamin in this mess in the first place.

"Jack, darling," called a voice, and the door to the study swung open.

Mina jumped to her feet. The woman was unmistakable. Everyone knew that Jack Townsend worked for Lady Agnes, the young widow of Hart Street. She was striking to look at, with dark hair and unusual height. It made Mina feel every inch a country mouse in comparison.

"Oh, pardon me, I didn't realize you had a guest." Lady Agnes smiled. "How do you do?"

Mina dropped into a curtsy.

"Not to worry. Lady Agnes, this is Miss Mina Sharpe." Townsend's pacing stopped to introduce her, but then started up again. "Miss Sharpe is in search of a wooden box with a heart-shaped lock."

Lady Agnes gave Mina an intrigued look, as if this search for a wooden box could very well render real treasure. "When you are finished here, won't you both take tea in the drawing room with me? Miss Sharpe, please join me. I'd love to hear more of this mystery, and I'm afraid Jack is miserable with details when he first takes on a case."

Mina curtsied again, and while she could keep her hands from trembling, her eyes fluttered at the unexpected invitation. "Yes, my lady, I would be honored."

"Good, I'll leave you to discuss your case. Jack will escort you down." With that, the young Widow of Hart Street vanished.

For her part, she didn't know what would be in the chest. The past year had done nothing but prove to her that everything she'd understood about her life was wrong. This wholly unexpected path that left her sitting in front of Jack Townsend had begun at her uncle's funeral. While sorting through his subsequent bequests, it was found that her uncle had never had a sibling. Her aunt, in bed with fever from the dread pneumonia that had felled her husband, whispered that she had not had a sibling either, but had taken in Mina and her brother out of the goodness of their hearts. But the goodness of a heart didn't stop a debt collector, and thus, what few possessions the children arrived with had been sold in order to pay for their keep.

But from whence had Mina and Benjamin come almost two decades before? From whom? All her aunt would say was that she regretted selling the wooden chest with the heart-shaped lock, for surely something wonderful had been hidden inside. It was desperation and a season of poverty and hunger that had pushed her aunt and uncle to sell the chest without first unlocking the treasure. Would it have been gold meant to help finance the raising of Benjamin and Mina? Or was it the kind of treasure that would help Benjamin and Mina answer all the questions they posed to each other in the evenings as they stared into their meager fire.

"Where did you last see the object?"

Mina's attention snapped back to Townsend. "I don't remember. Well over a decade ago." He continued to pepper her with peculiar questions, and she did her best to answer. Everything from her erstwhile aunt and uncle, to the village where she had grown up, just northwest of London. Exhausting every avenue of kin and relations and parish records, Mina wondered if next he would ask her favorite color.

Finally, the interview ended and Mr. Townsend—as he had graciously clarified that he was more accustomed to being mister when conducting business—escorted Mina to the drawing room. Mina belatedly wondered how much the finder's fee would be, and knew she needed to ask, but when they walked into the drawing room where Lady Agnes sat with another very tall woman, a Miss Persephone, the thought flew out of Mina's head.

Miss Persephone was as striking as Lady Agnes, tall and broad, with high cheekbones and kohl outlining her eyes, even though it was daytime. Mina shrank into her chair, not knowing how to address these two women who carried themselves with such confidence. Lady Agnes's hair was thick and lustrous, piled in beautiful curls around her head. Miss Persephone's was thicker, but just as artfully arranged. But both women did their best to pull her into polite conversation, and Mina settled enough to accept Lady Agnes's gracious hospitality. Miss Persephone seemed genuinely interested in Mina's answers, and her gentle smile was all Mina needed for encouragement.

The tea was better than Mina had tasted anywhere else, thick and dark as roasted chestnuts. By the time Mina was ready to leave, it occurred to her that no one had questioned her lack of chaperone. Everything else under the sun had been discussed, but not a single person had asked why she was going about London by herself. She fixed her bonnet and donned her gloves, puzzling over the very strange house in Marylebone, one that she had promised to return to in a fortnight for another cup of darkly brewed tea.

"Would you mind if I escorted you home?" Miss Persephone asked, joining her in the hallway and donning her own bonnet. Miss Persephone towered over her even more than Mina had predicted while they'd been seated.

"I don't doubt that it would be quite out of your way," Mina said. They hadn't much money, and her brother did what he could to make them comfortable, but it meant they were far from fashionable central London.

"I wouldn't insist, normally," Miss Persephone said, pulling on her gloves. "Yet, here you are without a chaperone. It will hardly do if you are looking to raise your rank."

Mina's hope that her chaperone-less status would go unnoticed evaporated. She scrambled to answer, but found she just opened and closed her mouth like a fish. She'd had a chaperone, as her brother had gone to London before her, sending for her only once he had been able to set up a proper household with a suitable matron, Mrs. Bushington.

Mrs. Bushington had been a proper widow, who had promptly dropped dead of an apoplexy, one day shortly after moving in with them. Hopefully, it hadn't been anything Mina had done, but her brother had not suggested a replacement as of yet, giving Mina a greater latitude than other young ladies.

"Not to worry, my dear, I'm the epitome of discretion." Miss Persephone gave her a winning smile.

"All right, then. But I promise you, it is quite a long walk." Mina finished pulling on her gloves.

"All the better for my girlish figure."

Miss Persephone was a delightful walking companion, and Mina found herself compelled to tell her all about Benjamin, from his secretary work for a gentleman, to the time he fell out of a tree trying to rescue her and still bore the scar across his eyebrow.

"Where will you start?" Agnes asked Jack. They sat in the library, lingering over a late night glass of port.

Jack had one leg slung over the side of a chair, his skirts draped like a fan. "The Dutchman, of course."

"Even though it's been so long since the girl has seen the box?" Agnes held her delicate glass up to the fire, admiring the deep ruby color of her spirits, turning the stem between her fingers as she did every night they took port.

"The Dutchman sees every object coming through the southern half of England. He'll either have it, or know where it went." Jack finished his glass and stood to take Agnes's. She downed hers and handed it off.

"What do you think is inside?" Agnes asked him.

Jack looked at her, trying to see her anew, as he had years ago. Her beauty, the clean lines of her jaw, the contrast of her dark hair to her pale face. The deep, abiding curiosity and the gentleness that made him fall in love with her. "Only memories by now; I'm sure someone has cracked it open. But well worth trying to find."

"The girl's hems were well worn."

"Were they?" Jack asked, as if he hadn't also noticed. He stowed the empty glasses on the drink cart for the maid to take down to the kitchens in the morning. They were fragile in his hand, as if he could snap the stems in half with hardly an effort.

"Miss Persephone sent a note, alerting me that the girl and her brother reside far from here. Quite the walk. Not a bad neighborhood, but not noteworthy."

Jack turned so he could better read his beloved's face. "These observations seem to be building to something specific."

Agnes pierced him with her gaze, in a way only she could. "She doesn't have the money, Jack. She can't afford you, let alone any assorted fees you may encounter along the way."

"Maybe I'll take this case for free." He wanted this job—a brother and sister together against the world? It seemed a dream to Jack, considering his own brother. To help them seemed like he was plucking sheer goodness out of the air.

"Ask," she whispered.

"It's not mine to ask for," Jack told her. In the years since they'd lived together, his beloved managed to gather around her a salon of sorts—bluestockings with convictions and pin money, men who thought more of ideas than chasing skirts—and they collected membership dues with the express purpose of helping those in need when they ran across them.

But, Jack didn't pay dues. Agnes paid them. Every month, a lump sat in his throat as they passed a basket, and Jack put nothing in. There were rare moments when their inequality was laid so bare: she had money, he did not. He knew she didn't mind paying, but he already lived at her behest. He lived in her house, with her servants, and his meager income could never catch up to the expense.

"This seems a noble cause, does it not?" she asked.

He couldn't look at her. But he could take action where she could not, and that had to count for something. She could save that money for a case he couldn't afford. "I can manage this one."

"How much will it cost us?" Benjamin asked. He was in his shirtsleeves, not bothering to pull on his coat for her. Not that he needed to, really, but if they were going to playact propriety, then he ought.

"I don't know," Mina said. "The topic was never broached." She'd meant to ask how much it cost, thought very hard about it, but with the strangeness of the experience, the awe she'd felt in the drawing room of the young widow of Hart Street, she'd forgotten entirely.

Benjamin groaned and ran his hands through his russet-colored hair. "How many times must I remind you that we are of limited means? You must ask about fees before you engage services."

His hands in his hair made her fingers itch to put her hands in her own hair. It was the compulsion of being twins, perhaps. Some of their neighbors had made strange comments about them over the years—that being twins was a bad omen, or that they had a supernatural connection to one another. If supernatural meant having a close friendship with one's brother, then yes, she was supernatural. Positively strange.

"Mister Townsend didn't mention it, so it didn't occur to me to do so, either. Perhaps what's in the chest will provide for us."

A haunted look came over Benjamin's dark eyes. "You cannot imagine that anything of value would be there. It's been at least a decade."

"But there wasn't a key, and Aunt Phillipa said it was locked," Mina mentioned hopefully.

"Do you think that would stop anyone? They would smash it to bits."

"It isn't fair," Mina said, slumping in the chair next to him. All those years, hours spent alone with Aunt Philippa, drying herbs from the garden, beating the dust out of curtains, polishing the floors and the silver, and never once did she mention a chest with a heart-shaped lock. Or her parentage. Or anything, truly. It was as if Aunt Phillipa had turned her entire childhood into a mirage, a fakery. All she had left was Benjamin, and all he had was her.

"Life's not fair, Min." Benjamin grabbed her hand. Both of their fingers were icy, given they couldn't afford coal. The weather hadn't turned yet, but Mina didn't want to think about what winter would bring.

THE DUTCHMAN WASN'T DUTCH. The story went that there had once been tulips planted nearby, or perhaps there had been tulips painted nearby, but either way, the sprawling brick building had stood for well over a century and rumor had it that its inhabitant had as well.

Inside was the detritus of London. Mudlarkers, traveling Romani, those in search of a few extra quid, all showed up here eventually. The Dutchman, whether he knew it or not, was Jack's best-kept secret, because he took in every treasure, every bit and bob, without ever asking its origins. The original owners were the losers of this game, but Jack had often come out the winner. Most of London never knew there was a game afoot.

"Fair Charlie!" Jack shouted as he entered the building. The mud floor kept it cold and dank inside, even if it was a rare sunny day out-of-doors. Jack wished he'd donned his trousers for this outing, forgetting how difficult it was to keep a skirt's hem out of this muck.

The large man came lumbering out from the labyrinthine shelves. "What's your luck today, Jack?"

"You know me, whatever I can make it. In search of a fairly large item this time, think you might help?"

The man's bushy gray eyebrows raised. He was not just tall, but large. One of his hands could span Jack's entire thigh. "What you wearing skirts for?"

"What, you just now using your eyeballs? Thought they were marbles you could sell for a ha'penny?"

His grunt was a signal for Jack to get on with it.

"A chest, about so big," Jack said, holding his hands out wide, the size of a chest that a person could carry all on their own, though it would be unwieldy. "Made of wood. Old—possibly very old. With a heart-shaped lock."

"How long ago?" Fair Charlie asked, his eyes on the ground, as if he were searching the shelves mentally.

"Likely a decade or more. But it came from outside of London, so it is possible it never came through here."

Fair Charlie scoffed. "I see everything that comes through. Naught to worry. I know the piece yer describing. But I don't have it." He lumbered over to the counter where more detritus was piled high. He sorted through a tray of small buttons and baubles.

"Fair enough. Might I ask where it went after your gentle hands caressed it?" Jack sauntered closer; he liked looking at what might have come in.

Fair Charlie snorted, which was as close as he got to laughter. Jack considered it a win.

"Gave it to Reese for repair. It was right falling apart at the seams."

"Reese over by the dairy?"

Fair Charlie moved past Jack, pulling up an empty wooden tray and leather satchel. He dropped broken buttons and odd bits into the leather satchel and the nicer baubles into the wooden tray. "Long ago, never got it back. Likely, he still has it."

"Reese hasn't finished a job in ages." Jack was thinking back to any good word he'd heard about Reese. He was a carpenter by trade, and a talented one at that. But years ago, he'd gotten a fever, and had never fully recovered.

"Don't I know it." Fair Charlie pulled out another tray, moving things with his hand, cataloging it in that mysterious head of his.

"Much obliged, then, Fair Charlie. I'll be on my way. Regards to the missus." Jack backed out of the dank building before the Dutchman could grunt in return.

It was strange to be amongst such a crowd of people and know no one. To walk the streets with no one to greet or exchange comments about the weather. It made her miss her old life, Aunt Phillippa and Uncle William, and her small but cozy village life.

Their maid-of-all-work, Penny, was at her heels, eyes wide and thin body tensed, as if every person they encountered would attack them both. She was a small thing, but strung together with tight muscle and sheer determination. Between them, Mina and Penny kept a clean household and a tidy larder. It wasn't much, but it was theirs. When Benjamin complimented them on a meal, or even the tidiness of their home, both of them felt pride. It wasn't all Mina wanted—to keep house for her brother—but it was something to hold onto while she figured out the new world she'd been thrust into.

The mild morning sun felt good on Mina's skin, and she was near to closing her eyes to enjoy it when Penny gasped. Mina turned her head, just in time for the warming, yeasty smell of fresh sweet buns to waft over. The sun, the aroma of baked goods, she really did close her eyes to let it roll through her senses. They hadn't had such a treat in weeks. Mina felt guilty—she'd had delights when she'd visited Jack Townsend a few weeks prior, but Benjamin hadn't and neither had Penny. Could they afford an indulgence like this today?

Mina felt a loyalty to Penny, as if she were more than a hired girl, but rather, some kind of relation. Mina had said as much to Benjamin one Sunday, as Penny waved goodbye to them for her half-day off of work to visit her mother. Benjamin smiled indulgently at her and told her she would never do as a wealthy man's wife.

"Oh!" Mina collided with a hard surface.

"Pardon me," a man said, his voice inflected by a French accent.

Mina looked up to see she had collided with the broad chest of an unusually handsome man. He had dark, curly hair—unruly really, escaping the confines of his hat—and warm, brown eyes. "My apologies," she managed to get out. "How very clumsy of me."

"Not at all, my fault entirely. I was distracted by the smell—"

"As was I," Mina interrupted, laughing in a very unladylike fashion. She shouldn't have interrupted him; Aunt Phillippa had told her that men didn't like young women who spoke out of turn. This was why she would live with Benjamin forever, or at least as long as he could support them both.

But the man laughed as well. "If we are both famished, should we not satisfy this hunger?"

A flutter danced in Mina's stomach, and Penny clutched her arm. "We couldn't possibly, but we do appreciate the offer."

His face softened, and he bowed his head, tweaking his hat. "Of course. I will not take up any more of your time. My apologies, miss."

Mina gave a shallow curtsy in return, unable to tear her eyes from his. Penny pulled her along. Once they were to the flower cart and well away from the curly-headed man, Penny squealed.

"So polite!"

"Penny!" Mina said, hoping to keep her voice down, despite the fact that she felt the same way.

"Do you think he comes to market often?" Penny stared after the man for so long that it was Mina's turn to yank her arm.

"London is so big, we'll likely never see him again." Mina gathered her thoughts and pulled the foolscap out of her pocket to look at her list of necessary items. She couldn't even read her own writing. "He was handsome, though."

"His hair!" Penny groaned.

"Penny. Focus on the task at hand."

"His chest was so broad! Do you think he was a tradesman? A gentleman wouldn't be so muscular."

"Penny!" Mina's hands were practically shaking from the amount of concentration she had to put into her list. Penny was saying aloud everything Mina was thinking. A tradesman would be within her reach.

A CARPENTER's house shouldn't have been in such woeful need of repair. Even Jack could tell the rain spout was clogged and the water damage was ruining the wall. That should've been shored up ages ago. Shit on toast, this family needed help. Jack knocked on the door. A square-jawed woman opened it, drying her chapped, red hands on her apron. Her skin was pale, not just from her ancestors, but from some other malady. Living as Jack had grown accustomed, seeing Agnes and her family laugh with each other, share meals, admire the luster of Agnes's hair, it was strange to see a person so dulled by life.

"Hullo. Here to see Mr. Reese."

The woman looked Jack up and down, no doubt noticing the finely tailored men's waistcoat, watch fob, and Jack's matching women's skirts. "And who ye be?"

"Jack Townsend. An old acquaintance, but here on professional business. The Dutchman referred me."

Recognition lit in her eyes, and suddenly her posture straightened. She ushered him in with a graceful sweep of her arm. No doubt the promise of money helped. "He's just in here, then." The woman walked ahead of him to the large drawing room. It showed signs of prosperity at one time, but no longer. The rug was threadbare, and while the room was stocked with well-made furniture, there was little else to recommend it. A hope chest easily three times the size of the one Jack was seeking sat squat under the window, half-carved. Likely another project never finished.

Reese sat in one of the four finely made chairs nearest to the hearth. An adolescent boy sat at his feet, whittling. Reese stared into the fire, nothing seeming to register. It was a shock to see a man so obviously infirm.

"Mr. Reese?" Jack said, swiping his hat off.

"May I take your hat and gloves, sir?" the boy asked, his voice still pitched high.

"No, thank you; I should be only a moment," Jack said before he thought. But, as Reese barely turned his head when Jack called his name, perhaps the boy was a better resource. "Wait a moment—" Jack called out, halting the boy's progress. "Perhaps this will take some time, please, if you would. What's your name?"

"Georgie," the boy answered, eyes wide.

"Thank you, Georgie. Much obliged."

Georgie crept forward and Jack kept talking. He handed off his hat, then set about fiddling with a button on his glove. "You see, Mr. Reese, I'm in search of a chest. It isn't terribly big. The size a grown person might carry in their arms, made of wood, likely quite old. The Dutchman said he entrusted it to you to repair its soft edges many years ago. Does such an object exist here in the house?"

Reese turned slowly towards Jack, but his eyes didn't seem capable of locking onto him at all.

"Ah, yes, and one more detail that might jog your memory: it has a heart-shaped lock, I believe. Very distinctive."

Georgie bounced on his heels at the mention of the lock. Jack turned to him under the pretense of handing off his second glove.

"Does such an object sound familiar?" Jack asked.

Georgie nodded, glancing over to Reese, no doubt his father, as if he could grant permission.

"Why don't you find it for me? I'll give you a sum for it, and take it off your hands." Jack would gladly overpay for the chest. He had enough blunt for that. And if anyone needed money, it was these people. He could help Miss Sharpe and the Reese family in one fell swoop, and be glad to do it.

Georgie scampered away, shoving Jack's hat and gloves at his mother, who appeared in the doorway.

"You'll pay a good sum," she said, her eyes hard.

Jack knew she'd noticed his expensive pocket watch. She was holding his beaver fur hat, so she knew that he was at least near wealth. "Gladly, madame."

She disappeared back into the other rooms and Jack sat down across from Reese. The man seemed to enjoy conversation, so Jack did what he excelled at: he talked. He mentioned the weather, the new building developments happening, the rumors of tearing down the Five Courts boxing amphitheater. Reese's eyes seemed to light up at the mention of buildings, so Jack kept on, forgoing any chatter about the King's lack of an heir.

Georgie's clomping footsteps echoed throughout the house long before the boy appeared. But when he did, his arms were full, taken up completely by the chest.

"This, then," Georgie said, gasping for breath, as he dropped it to the floor in front of Jack. A thin sheen of sweat shone across the boy's forehead.

Jack inspected the chest. The wood looked soft, no doubt kept in a dank sort of place. There was an unintelligible carving on the side, and the lock was not heart-shaped, though it was easy to see why one might remember it to be so. No, the wood was carved into a heart shape surrounding the lock. The lock itself was naught but a simple design.

"I do believe it is," Jack said, hauling the object up onto his lap. It was in poor repair. A blacksmith could easily fix the corners, and the bottom was far too soft to hold anything of weight. The cost of repair, even taking it to a friend like Os Worley, was more than Jack could afford, in addition to what he would have to pay Reese.

But, if he used the funds from the salon, then he could easily help both the Sharpe siblings and the Reese family. It was just a matter of swallowing his pride. Those others had the money, wanted to help those less fortunate, and while this wasn't a dire circumstance, it was one of heavy emotional weight. If only Jack could accept some help.

Shit on toast, he hated taking Agnes's money for his own work. But it wasn't her money, not really. It was the salon's, and this was the reason they collected it in the first place. Fine.

Mrs. Reese came into the room, again drying her red, chapped hands on her apron. "Well now, that does look like something Mr. Reese would have repaired prior to his sickness."

"Indeed." This woman clearly worked herself to the bone to provide for her family and care for her ill husband and young child. She needed assistance and was likely just as stubborn as Jack about taking it. She'd gladly work in exchange for a fee, but Jack would bet that she wasn't the sort to accept charity. "I'll give you four pounds for it."

Georgie coughed. It was a princely sum for an unrepaired piece. Probably what they earned in a year. But the woman showed no signs of surprise or pleasure.

"Done. Four pounds. Georgie, get the gentleman's hat and gloves." She gave her son a stern nod.

Jack stood, fished out bank notes from his pocket and handed them over. "Georgie seems to be quite helpful."

Mrs. Reese's eyes cut towards Jack, full of suspicion. She smoothed the paper in her hands. "He's a good lad."

"I have a note I would like to get to a young lady, whose family is inquiring after this particular item. Would you allow him to deliver the message? For a shilling?" A shilling was far more than carrying a message would ever cost, but Jack wanted them to have it.

"How far would he travel?" Mrs. Reese asked, folding the money over once and securing it into her pocket.

"North London, to some lodging not unlike this. Lovely people." Jack couldn't promise they would tip the boy, but the enticement was there.

"Fine, then."

Georgie returned with the gloves and hat. Jack took them, putting on the hat, but holding the gloves. He fished in his pockets for some foolscap and a pencil he always kept on his person.

PENNY AND MINA were dusting when a boy arrived carrying a missive from Jack Townsend.

Miss Sharpe,
  The chest has been found, but is in poor repair. I am taking it to Mr. Worley's smithy in Paddington today. I shall remain there for some time; please come if you are able.
  Jack Townsend

Mina pulled off her cap and apron and sleeves and ran into Benjamin's office. She scribbled a note for him to meet her at the blacksmith's as soon as he was able. She folded it, not caring if the boy—or anyone else—read it. She gave the boy instructions on how to find Benjamin and then sent him on his way with a day-old roll and a bruised plum. She supposed it was better than a candle-stub, because that's all she had to offer in payment for his efforts.

With the boy on his way to Benjamin, she pinned on a bonnet, not bothering to fix her hair or even check for smudges in the looking glass.

"Shouldn't I be going with you, miss?" Penny reminded her, taking off her apron.

It wasn't always safe for a woman walking alone, but Mina would be on well-traveled streets in the middle of the day. The excitement was too much. "No time!" she shouted, dashing out the door, with no hope that Penny could keep up.

At first, Mina desperately wished for money to hire a hack to take her to the blacksmith's. Walking as fast as she might without appearing to run, Mina was now in the thick of Town, dodging people and vendors and obstinate horses. There was traffic on Holborn, which was when she revised her wish for a hack. She'd be stuck in it for hours if she'd had the coin for it.

Instead, her thin-soled boots danced and slipped along, barely landing before the next step was taken. It felt strange to be so excited about the chest. She had no idea what was in it, or if it would mean anything at all. Perhaps she would receive an old wooden box, and she would take it home to Benjamin, and then they would have it. An old box. But maybe it would be the gold Benjamin hoped for. Maybe it would contain a journal from their parents. Something to mark their heritage.

Mina crossed over a small bridge, which brought her officially into Paddington. She asked directions outside of a tavern for Mr. Worley's smithy, and was guided to a large building with a yard full of chickens.

Something about the chickens in the yard made her feel at ease, as if there was a touch of village life here in the middle of

London. She made her way to the building, and when she entered the door, the sudden darkness blinded her.

"Hello?" she called, hating that she sounded so timid. She wondered if Benjamin had gotten her note, and how soon he would arrive.

"Miss Sharpe, thank you for being so prompt." Jack Townsend appeared at her side and guided her in as her eyes adjusted. The heat inside felt welcoming.

"Of course," she said, feeling unbalanced as she stepped forward on the soft dirt floor. "I'm thrilled you were able to locate the chest so quickly." Her eyes adjusted enough to see Jack Townsend smile at her. That's when she realized they were of a height. It made him seem less intimidating somehow.

"I took the liberty of bringing it to the blacksmith's due to its state of disrepair. I wanted you to see it before he reinforces the corners."

Mina wrung her hands. The extra expense of a blacksmith's work was decidedly not within their means. Benjamin would once again sink his head in his hands, and she would know it was her fault.

"Let me open the doors," a low, accented voice said. Before long, large barn doors slid open, revealing the tall, broad-shouldered blacksmith, wearing a leather apron and no shirt sleeves. His curly brown hair fell this way and that, and Mina startled.

"Miss Mina Sharpe, may I introduce you to the blacksmith, Mr. Jean Fabron. He is the journeyman to the master blacksmith, Mr. Worley, but both assure me that Mr. Fabron is more than capable of these repairs." Jack Townsend all but melted into the background.

The broad-chested man with curly hair stepped toward her, framed by the new light. It was the same man from the market, except somehow he seemed even more handsome. In all of Mina's stories of Greek and Roman mythologies, of Vulcan hammering away at his forge, he was never like this Mr. Fabron. She found she couldn't speak.

"Pleasure to make your acquaintance, Miss Sharpe." He gave her an easy grin that made her weak in the knees. Hearing him say the word pleasure in his mild accent didn't help matters, either.

His arms were covered in coal dust and sweat, and she should have been disgusted, but it was very hard to be disgusted when looking at the strength of them. A flash of wondering what it would feel like to anchor oneself in such strong arms skittered through her mind, but Mina pushed it away. Family obligation brought her here, and she must remain focused. Benjamin needed her to do her part for their tiny family of two.

"I do apologize. Mr. Fabron, thank you for, er—" Why was she here? "Inspecting the chest. Box. Item." Her cheeks heated, and it wasn't from the forge.

"Of course." He opened his mouth again, as if he were going to say more, but he didn't. Instead, he gestured over to the far wall, where a workbench held the newly found chest.

"This is it?" Mina asked, as she followed the instruction of his gesture.

Jack Townsend appeared at her side. "Indeed. Would you like to inspect it first, and then we may discuss the repairs needed?"

"I have sent for my brother to come as well. He is best to discuss any of the specifics." She meant the word money, but she couldn't bring herself to say it.

The chest was taller than she thought it would be, but then, she'd not had a good picture of it in her mind. She took off her gloves. There was something about it, the promise of family, as if it might restore some previously missing piece of her life, if only she could touch this much-sought-after relic of her past. Skimming her fingers along it at first, she found the wood was soft, as if she could carve into it with her fingernail. The lid was flat, and she ran her hand along the smooth, sanded surface. She opened the lid, but it clattered to the side, as the hinges were clearly broken. Inside, there was nothing.

"It's empty." She hadn't expected jewels or treasure, but she had hoped for something. A clue: a blanket, a Bible, even a simple button. Anything.

"Almost. If you would allow me, miss." The blacksmith came to stand next to her. He smelled of sweat and leather, and while it wasn't pleasant, she would not freely say it was unpleasant.

She stepped aside. He took the handle of a hammer and pushed down on the inside of the chest, right near the corner. The floor of the chest immediately popped up on the opposite side. Mina gasped.

"You see, there is a false bottom," Mr. Fabron said. "There is not much inside, but I did not want to touch it with my dirty hands."

She stared at his dirty hands for a moment, her body churning through things she hadn't time to think. Instead of speaking, Mina tried to reach down inside the chest but found she was too short.

"Here, miss," Jack Townsend said, supplying an upside-down crate for her to stand on.

"Thank you." Finally of an appropriate height, she lifted out the false bottom, revealing a cache of linens. There were two infant gowns, one beautiful, one hastily made. A few cloths, embroidered with purple thread depicting thistles in one corner, another embroidered with a theme of sweet peas, delicate white thread knotted to depict the tiny flowers. Mina took each one out and examined it with reverence. She held them close to her body, tucking each one in her arm, not wanting to set them down on the workbench. When the end came, she smoothed her hand across the true bottom.

In the shifting light, she saw pencil markings. "I need more light," she exclaimed.

"Why?" Jack Townsend said, raising up to his tiptoes in an effort to see.

Mr. Fabron was already whisking the chest off of the workbench and out into the chicken yard's full sun.

"There's something written on the bottom!" Mina hastened down from her crate, not bothering to use Jack Townsend's hand for balance. She ran to the chicken yard.

"What is it?" Jack Townsend asked, following after her.

Mina ran to Mr. Fabron, her breath catching. In pencil, written on the true bottom, was a treasure. The letters were not in the florid penmanship of a well-educated hand, but rather, in a hurried scratch of someone who knew their letters and only a bit more.

Wilhelmina Sharpe, Benjamin Sharpe
Born of
June Janssen Sharpe and Benjamin Sharpe of Sapiston

"Then how did we get to Sudbury?" Mina asked.

"Is that a riddle?" Jack Townsend asked, his forehead creasing as he frowned.

"I should wait until my brother arrives, so that he may look this over as well. I would hate for anything to be destroyed before he sees it."

"Destroyed?" Mr. Fabron sounded insulted. "No one will destroy anything."

"Let's hope not," Benjamin's voice carried across the yard.

"You made it!" Mina felt a kind of thrill inside of her, as if they were on the precipice of something. That even though there was no great treasure, there was something for them: their parents.

"Of course, this is important." Benjamin made his way through the front gate, dodging chickens. "This is it, yes?"

Jack Townsend stepped forward, and suddenly he seemed so small next to her twin. "It is. However, you'll note that it is in poor repair. Mr. Fabron believes he can reinforce it without damaging the original design."

"And look," Mina said, thrusting the linens at Benjamin. "These must have been ours."

"Ah yes," Benjamin said, pulling up the beautiful infant gown, and then the less well-made one. "Mine and yours."

"Everyone knows I was the expected one, and you were uninvited," Mina said, repeating the old tease. Benjamin had been the smaller of the two of them, but he had grown much taller afterwards.

Benjamin smiled and returned the gowns. "I'm the extra pudding at the end of a meal. Impossible to resist. And ho, what's this?" He peered into the chest that Mr. Fabron still held. "Is that?" Benjamin looked up at her.

Mina nodded. "Those are our parents."

Benjamin reached out and clasped her hand. She wanted to twirl in a circle. It was silly how such a small piece of information might be so transforming, but to Mina, it was. They had parents.

"So how did we get to Sudbury?" Benjamin asked. Mr. Fabron chuckled.

"Miss Sharpe asked the very same thing," Jack Townsend said.

"I don't know, but it's a place to start," Mina said.

"That must be getting heavy. I do apologize; may I assist you?" Benjamin asked Mr. Fabron, as if just now seeing him.

"No trouble," Mr. Fabron said. "But may I give you my proposal for repairs?"

The small company returned to the workbench, and the blacksmith pointed out the corners where he would reinforce the joinery. Some internal slats had cracked and needed replacing. The carvings on the side were unintelligible, and would be smoothed over. But the heart carving around the lock could be repaired and even emphasized. The hinges would be replaced, and a key would be made.

"All that sounds very sensible," Benjamin said, but the tone of his voice made Mina's heart fall. She knew what came next. "But I'm afraid I don't have the coin for such extensive work."

Jack Townsend stepped forward. "If I may, I have a fund that I may use if I find a case of particular need. I would like to split some of the costs with you, if you would allow it, Mr. Sharpe. It's no trouble, and indeed, is the entire reason the fund exists."

Benjamin shifted. Mina could tell he was about to say no. He said that they'd relied on too much charity already in their lives, that he could provide for them. And this chest would slowly fall apart in their flat, and those pencil scratches would fade to nothing.

"Yes," Mina said, raising up on her tiptoes. She couldn't allow Benjamin to toss away the only relic of their past. "Yes, please, we would gladly accept your aid, Mr. Townsend."

Benjamin looked askance, but Mina ignored him. Mr. Fabron looked to Mr. Townsend. "I may be able to keep costs down. But I should hope that we might have a time when we may all come together after it is repaired?"

Mr. Townsend's face split with a smile. His eyes glittered as he looked at Mina, as if he were already planning schemes well into the future. "Of course. Lady Agnes regularly hosts a salon. When the chest is ready, perhaps we may all gather again, if that is acceptable?"

Benjamin looked between the two men and then to Mina. It was clear he knew something else was afoot, and didn't appreciate being ignorant of it, but Mina would tell him that evening. Would she tell him of her meeting with Mr. Fabron in the market?

MINA HAD WORKED every night on the embroidery on her nicest day dress. Lady Agnes was known for having an excellent artistic touch with such things, and Mina wanted to show her own skills. Or, at least, so she said aloud to Penny and Benjamin. Penny always looked at her slyly, but didn't complain taking over the rest of the darning in the evenings as Benjamin read aloud to them by the fire.

Now that Mina and Benjamin were at the townhouse in Marylebone again, where a peal of shimmering laughter floated down the staircase, Mina's heart tripped faster. Had it been a mistake to embroider her skirts so ostentatiously? It had looked marvelous at home, but out in public, she was surely too shabby to draw such attention to herself.

Mr. Fabron would be here. The blacksmith with curly hair and wide palms and competent arms. And she desperately wanted him to notice her, and not speak solely to her brother about money.

Benjamin looked up at the staircase. A peal of laughter was not a polite way to engage, as it showed lack of control, but Mina loved it. The idea they would be in a room of people so fully happy as to laugh with abandon seemed magical.

The footman took their hats and gloves, and a butler escorted them up. Benjamin squeezed Mina's arm to his and whispered, "Don't be nervous."

She squeezed his right back. They arrived at the drawing room where Mina had taken tea many weeks previous, a time that seemed so far away. It was crowded with far more people than Mina anticipated.

Miss Persephone was the culprit of the laughter. She stood nearest to the door, holding a tea cup and making eyes at a man a foot shorter. Lady Agnes sat in the blue velvet chair, presiding over the tea and more sedate conversation. Jack Townsend sat next to her, and near the window was Mr. Fabron, amidst a few others she didn't know.

The butler announced them, and Lady Agnes stood to usher them over. Mina curtsied and Benjamin bowed, but Mina felt the absence of finishing lessons. The rest of their company was not so elegant that they were out of place, but they were all so self-assured. Their sense of belonging and rightness was intimidating. How did one find such certainty?

"Before we conduct your business, please let me introduce you to our company," Lady Agnes said. "These are friends, and also members of an informal salon we hold here. Misfits and plotters, every one."

Benjamin chuckled at the idea of it, and they were well-received. Mr. Fabron elected to separate himself from his company—Mr. Os Worley, Mr. Fabron's master blacksmith, as well as the intriguing Mrs. Worley, London's championess prizefighter.

They met a well-dressed poet, the owner of a factory with radical labor ideas, a viscountess, and a painter. It was rather dizzying to be amongst such an eclectic gathering, but Mina appreciated their warm greetings.

Mr. Fabron was quiet, but always nearby, and after they'd had some tea, he brought forth the chest. His coat seemed tight as he carried it across the room, and Mina averted her eyes. She couldn't be seen showing such open appreciation. Benjamin seemed to note her interest.

"As you can see," Mr. Fabron said, pointing to the iron reinforced corners, "I've used some basic bracing to maintain its form. The wood will continue to warp over time as it ages. It will expand and contract with the seasons, but it should maintain its shape for a long time. I've had to reinforce the bottom as well, and instead of making it smaller, I've added more room to the ah—" He glanced around the room, noting the attention of everyone in the gathering. "—the extra compartment."

"So the piece with the writing on it is gone?" Benjamin asked.

"Not at all," Jean said. He pulled a key out of his waistcoat pocket and handed it to Mina.

The key was ornate, small, but beautiful. The rounded end was filigreed, and Mina couldn't help but run her fingers over the smooth, intricate design.

"Will you do the honors, Miss Sharpe?" Mr. Fabron asked.

Mina did her best not to blush. She shifted forward to reach the lock. It slid in without halting, and the mechanism worked with a satisfying click.

The lid sprang free, and Mina lifted it, testing the new hinges. She gave Mr. Fabron an encouraging smile, which he returned. Benjamin cleared his throat.

"May I see?" he asked, pushing Mina aside, toward Mr. Fabron.

"Brothers," she said, and the whole company laughed. All except Mr. Townsend.

Benjamin pushed the false bottom down in one corner and it sprang up in the next, just as it had before. He lifted it out of the way, and there it was, their prized possession, the names of their parents. Benjamin touched it with his hands.

"I did some research," Jack Townsend said, catching Mina's gaze. "Both Sapiston and Sudbury have large Flemish communities. Given the maiden name of your mother, Janssen, it is probable that is why you might have been transferred to Sudbury for care."

"Thank you," Benjamin whispered.

Mina watched his eyes go glassy, and felt her heart fill. She loved that her brother was an emotional man, his love for his family so clear and evident to all. He blinked back the tears, and grabbed Mina's hand.

"It's a start," she said. They had their baby clothes back at home. Proof that they were expected–even if two were not expected. There had been love. They had been wanted.

"With the addition of the metal reinforcements, the chest is much heavier than before. Would you allow me to drive it to you later this week? Perhaps I may call on Miss Sharpe while I am there?"

Mr. Fabron was asking Benjamin, but his eyes never left Mina's. The question snapped Benjamin out of his reverie. "Of course, if that is agreeable to Mina."

"Indeed," she said, once again fighting a blush staining her cheeks. It felt as if the whole room held their collective breath, watching the drama play out in front of them.

"Oh, for heaven's sake, people, talk amongst yerselves," the lady prizefighter said, saving Mina from expiring from embarrassment on the spot.

The murmurs of the crowd built higher, and both twins were given the time to control their emotions.

Jack Townsend slipped over next to Benjamin.

"I cannot express how thankful I am to you," Benjamin said. "I hope that in my gratitude, you will understand that I may need to make payment in installments. I hope that doesn't—"

Jack Townsend held up a hand. "Not to worry, Mr. Sharpe. The salon has already decided to cover all costs. It is rare in this life that we get to engineer a happy ending, and everyone here feels honored to help you find your origins."

Mina felt Mr. Fabron shift next to her as Jack Townsend's gaze landed on him.

"I hope you shall keep us informed about what happens next." Jack Townsend gave them all an enigmatic smile and excused himself.

"I cannot linger," Benjamin said. "My employer is still in need of me this evening."

"I am happy to escort Miss Sharpe home," Mr. Fabron volunteered. Benjamin's face tightened at the offer.

"Thank you, but—" Mina loved that the blacksmith wanted to spend time with her, but she could not go unchaperoned. She and her brother had not discussed her interest in Mr. Fabron, nor had they addressed the idea of any suitor.

"Are you heading out that way, Mr. Fabron?" Miss Persephone sauntered over. "How curious. I was hoping to go there myself. I'd be happy to chaperone Miss Sharpe on the drive. You are driving, aren't you?"

Benjamin's expression shifted to amused. "Very well. If Lady Agnes vouches for Miss Persephone, I'm happy to leave you in her capable hands." He stood, finding himself very much at eye level with the towering Miss Persephone. He bowed, and Miss Persephone sank into a beautiful curtsy.

Feeling awkward about starting a new conversation with Mr. Fabron, Mina set about restoring the chest to rights.

"Are you pleased with it?" Mr. Fabron asked her. "You haven't said."

His question caught her aback. "Of course I am. Your craftsmanship is excellent."

"I was worried about making it larger and heavier than before. It isn't as easily carried."

Miss Persephone settled on the sofa where Benjamin had been. She looked in the other direction to give them privacy.

"But you restored it to its real function. The lid once again serves. The lock has a key." She held up the beautiful object, as if to remind him.

He traced the engraved heart surrounding the lock. "I did my best to ensure the heart remained visible. I thought you would like that."

"I do. It will make me think of my parents. I should like to have known them."

"Family is important," Mr. Fabron said.

"I only have my brother."

"Family is more than just who carries your blood," Mr. Fabron said. "Family are those you rely on. Those who rely on you." His eyes cast about the room, settling on the master blacksmith and his wife. "Those are my family. And others."

Mina shook her head, feeling suddenly shy.

"If you do not wish to share, do not feel as if you should," he said gently.

"It's just," Mina looked up, his beautiful brown eyes warm and soft like a velvet button. "I don't know anyone."

Mr. Fabron chuckled. "That is more easily fixed. I would be happy to introduce you around. We are an unlikely bunch."

"I'd like that," Mina said, forcing herself to keep his gaze and not stare down at her hands. She liked him. She liked meeting new people.

She liked that suddenly, the future rolling out in front of her looked beautiful and full. That perhaps, someday, her household might not just be her brother and their maidservant. That she might have a house full of family, and those she called family. And no one would ever doubt where they belonged.

Edie Cay writes happily-ever-afters for relatable misfits. Her story, "A Rarefied Gift," employs Jack Townsend, one of the protagonists of her third novel, *A Lady's Finder*. If you want to read more about characters who don't quite fit during Regency London, start with *A Lady's Revenge,* book one in the When the Blood is Up series. To meet Os Worley, Bess Abbott, and Jean Fabron, read *The Boxer and the Blacksmith,* book two. Don't forget Jack's novel, book three, *A Lady's Finder,* and then read *A Viscount's Vengeance,* which publishes on March 1, 2023. For more about Edie, follow her on social media, Facebook, Instagram, Twitter, or subscribe to her newsletter for exclusive content.

THE SHELL
BY REBECCA D'HARLINGUE

AMSTERDAM, 1679

I hadn't expected Pieter to look into the bed linens cupboard. What husband would do such a thing? In all of our twenty years of marriage, he had never had the need. As in the homes of everyone I know, only I, the wife, remove and return things to those shelves. I always put out the clean linens on the days when the maid is to refresh the bedclothes.

But Pieter did open the cupboard, and what he found disturbed him.

Lest your imagination carry you to something shameful, let me hasten to explain. What Pieter found were some drawings which I had placed on the shelves, because they were the perfect size for the pages, and because I had believed that no one else would ever see them. My husband immediately assumed I was the artist, and so I was. Before we wed, I had been an engraver of maps, as had my father and two brothers. Our work was not original. We copied a map onto the copper plates for printing, but you can surely understand that without a certain skill in drawing, this could not be properly accomplished. Especially in the elaborate cartouches and decorative elements of a map, our own artistry came into play.

The papers stored in the cupboard, however, were not maps, but drawings of a shell from different perspectives and against various backgrounds. Some of the papers showed the smooth oval of the back of the shell, with the slightest of ridges crossing it horizontally. The opening of the shell was depicted on some pages, showing the cone shape at the bottom and the rest of the shell ascending from it in a half-circle sunrise. On other sketches, the spiral at the edge of the cone was visible, revealing far more complexity than one at first perceived.

Most of the drawings had no color, but some did. I recalled the many times my map colorist friend, Anneke, and I spent hours trying to get the precise shade of the shell correct. It is hard to describe the exact hue. Apricot, but paler. The early dawn reflected in the canals' waters. A touch of the pink of a young child's face. Anneke and I were never quite satisfied with our results, though sometimes we came close to the truth.

Once, I placed the shell on a table with flowers that almost approached its color. Another time, I laid it on a dark green piece of velvet and tried to capture the contrast between the nap of the fabric and the smooth sheen of the shell, but that is very difficult with watercolors, which were all that Anneke and I had. I imagined my shell on a faraway beach, and I designed fantastic-looking trees in the distance. In one painting, a pair of hands is holding the shell. A man's hands.

None of these would, I think, on their own have caused Pieter much perturbation. It was the other drawing that he found—of a man with a square jaw, curling hair, smooth cheeks, and large eyes, which seemed to cause his disquietude.

I hadn't tried to color this image, for I didn't think I could ever perfect the blue of the eyes or the gold of the hair, and that failure would be too jarring. The likeness would simply have to remind me of its subject, and my mind could conjure the shades.

Pieter correctly guessed this was Jacob, though they had never met. Before ever I knew Pieter, I had loved Jacob. Although we had not told our parents, he had promised we would wed when he returned from Batavia. He had signed onto a ship in hopes of getting enough money to set us up in our own home. But Jacob never came back. His shipmate had appeared at my parents' house one day, two years after Jacob had left, and told me that my love had died on the return journey. He related how much Jacob had spoken of me, and how fondly. He gave me the gift that Jacob had bought for me in that far-off land. The shell. The object I had drawn and painted so often; the shell whose representations I had kept all of these years.

I had told Pieter about Jacob when he asked me to marry him. I loved Pieter, and he deserved to know there had been another man in my life. He understood and even thanked me for telling him. It was hard for him to know that he was not the first one I had feelings for, but he said he was happy he would be the last. He urged me to forget the past and look to the future, to the happiness he and I would build. But Pieter asked that we never speak of Jacob again.

We never did, though sometimes Anneke would mention Jacob to me. She had spent so many hours helping me try to get the color for the shell correct. She had felt my sorrow and she knew the drawings helped me to heal. She was the only person I could talk to about Jacob. I would say that he was in the past, that I loved Pieter very much, and who knows whether Jacob and I could have made such a happy marriage together. Besides, if I hadn't married Pieter, we wouldn't have our children, Hendrick and Deborah, now almost grown. Granted, I might have had other children with Jacob, but I could not imagine my life without my precious son and daughter. They know nothing of Jacob. To speak to them of him would seem somehow a betrayal of their father.

I had never told Pieter of Jacob's gift, but then he found the papers.

"Why are all of these drawings of a shell hidden away with a picture of a man?"

"That is Jacob," I said, looking directly at my husband. "The shell was a gift from him, brought to me by his shipmate."

"Are the drawings recent?"

"No, Pieter! They are from before I met you."

"Then why have you kept them? Do they still have meaning for you?"

I told him, "They do not." I do not like to lie to my husband, but it seemed the kinder thing to do.

For days, I could see that his discovery weighed on Pieter. He was the kind, patient husband and father as always, but he did not joke with me or the children. At the evening meal he did not ask each of us about our day, as had been his wont. Indeed, he spoke little, and he seemed unsure of himself, hesitating before expressing his thoughts on even the most common subjects. One day, he asked me whether I still had the shell, and I told him it must have been mislaid years ago. This did not seem to cheer him as much as I had hoped it would, to be told I had cared so little for the object my first love had given me.

At night, when we were in our bed alcove, he did not seem to hold me with the same warmth as before. I don't think he wished to punish me, but I felt it as such. He seemed somehow timid, as though he could not get it out of his mind that he was not the first to claim a place in my heart, even though the other had been decades ago.

Pieter was the postmaster for the Antwerp sorting office, which handled correspondence between Amsterdam and Belgium, France, Spain, and Portugal, and when he began to seem a bit on edge, I asked him whether there was a particular problem with the post, but he said no. I believed him, for I had never seen him out of sorts over anything at work. Pieter was a calm man. The only conclusion I could come to was that he was still troubled by the drawings.

I did not know what to do. I did what I could to show him my love, but since in all of our marriage, we had not spoken of Jacob except on the day that Pieter had found the drawings, it seemed unnatural to do so now. I could not simply say that he should not worry about Jacob, that it was he, Pieter, whom I loved.

One evening, he seemed particularly saddened, and when pressed, he confessed he had been to the docks that day to deal with a problem for a shipment to Spain. A ship returning from Batavia was also docked, and it put him in mind of Jacob, the shell, and the drawings I had clearly painstakingly done. Although I had feared the idea of Jacob was still pervading his thoughts, his admission surprised me. All of my subsequent assurances seemed to have little effect.

The next day, while Pieter was at the post office, I went to see Anneke. We no longer visited as often as we once did. She had become a successful map colorist, and was much in demand, and she had children of her own to care for. I had given up my engraving work when I married, but caring for my family kept me busy. Still, I knew I could go to her, and she, after all, had been with me when I had made the drawings all those years ago, trying to hold on to some small part of Jacob.

I felt some guilt in sharing with her what was happening between Pieter and me. It seemed disloyal to tell her of his sentiments without his knowledge. Still, I hoped that Anneke might have an idea.

"I didn't know you still had the drawings. Why did you keep them?" There was surprise, and perhaps censure, in her tone, and I turned away.

"I don't know, Anneke," I said quickly. "The question is, what am I to do now?"

"Do you know, before I married Daniel, he suspected I had feelings for another man?" I spun round to stare at my friend.

"No! That wasn't true, was it?"

"It was, for a brief time," Anneke said softly, then she added almost defiantly, "but I firmly denied it to Daniel. The slight deception was done from love, and we have had a happy marriage. You must do something to remove the doubt that Pieter now feels."

"But what can I do?"

"You must destroy the pictures, and Pieter must know that you have done so."

That had crossed my mind, but I had been reluctant to take that final step. Anneke's declaration felt like a slap, but I saw that she was right. That night, after Hendrick and Deborah had gone to their beds, I asked Pieter to leave the book he was reading and to come with me.

I led him to the linen cupboard and removed the drawings. I then silently walked over to the hearth and, one by one, fed the papers to the fire. I saw each page curl at the edges, then I watched the flames slowly move toward the center, engulfing the image. Page after page was consumed, the simple drawings and the colored ones. There was the drawing of the hands, Jacob's hands, holding the shell, and I remembered those hands caressing me. I kept the drawing of Jacob until last, as though those few extra moments of its existence in the world could offer some small comfort. Finally, I laid it on the flames, and it was as though I was losing him again, this time to fire rather than water. I lowered my head toward the blaze, the heat somehow giving me a final connection to my lost love. As I rose again, Pieter studied my face, and I struggled to keep it tranquil. Neither of us said a word, but when Jacob's face was turned to ash, I walked into Pieter's arms, and we embraced.

MANY MONTHS HAVE PASSED since I consigned the drawings to the fire. Pieter and I are as we were before, and I am a happy wife and mother. Now and then, I feel a pang to think that the pictures are no more, though in truth, I had rarely looked at them. It seems knowing that they were there, waiting for me, had been enough.

In our home there is a loft, situated between the sides of the peak of our roof. It is a tiny room, and only I ever bother to climb the winding stairs to reach it. A wife has more time to explore the family's domain than does a husband, and more interest. A man has a wider world to probe, but a woman's expeditions are limited to scouting every corner and cubby of her home.

Some things are stored haphazardly in the loft. My gaze, at times, falls on some drawings that my young children made, and I must admit they display no early talent. I hold up the christening costume that both my children and my husband wore, and I wonder that they were ever so small. The shirts that

THE SHELL

Pieter and I each wore on our wedding night are carefully preserved, waiting to dress our corpses on our deathbeds, as is the custom.

In the corner is an old box bed which was left by the last inhabitants of the house. We have never used it, but neither have we gotten rid of it, since it would be so difficult to remove. Taking it down the stairs would be impossible. We would have to use the hook and pulley on the outside of the house to lower it, and that is more trouble than it is worth. Below the opening for the bed is a small door, though the design is such that it would be easy to miss. But I know it is there, and within it is a wooden chest I discovered in the early weeks of our marriage.

The chest is about an arm's length long, the width and height less. It fits snugly inside the bed cupboard's compartment, and you must angle it a certain way to remove it. It is clearly very old. I have no idea who it belonged to, nor how it came to be hidden here. I am certain that Pieter does not know of its existence. The chest has carvings on the front and sides. On one side there is what appears to be a face, but in the outline of what looks to be a shield. Along the bottom of the front there is a row of carvings in the shape of church windows. Above that are three sections. The two side pictures seem to be flowers. In the middle is a heart, and in the middle of the heart is a hole for a key.

The chest intrigued me from the start, and after I first discovered it, I returned to it most every day. The more I looked at the chest, the more perplexed I became. From the outside it looked deeper than it did when one peered in. I had heard of false bottoms, but I could find no way to lift it, as my fingers were too large to get hold of the inside edge. I finally inserted a knife along the sides, and I pried the bottom up, revealing a shallow space.

The chest was empty when I found it, and it seemed to cry out to be filled. Something kept me from doing that, however, for if someone else discovered the chest, things inside would invite exploration, and I had already decided what I wished to hide beneath the false bottom.

I hid Jacob's shell there all those years ago. I do not like to lie to my husband, but I did deceive him when I led him to believe that I did not know its whereabouts.

From time to time, when no one else is home, I climb the twisting steps to the loft. I do not rush to the chest. I look around, seeing the remnants of our lives that have been consigned to this place, out of sight and mind to everyone but me. The things I see often carry happy memories.

Then I walk the few steps to the bed cupboard. I put my hand on the bed and wonder about those who found their rest there. I kneel upon the floorboards and open the door below. I reach out for the chest and pull it toward me, sometimes forgetting that I must hold it just so, or it will be caught by the borders of the door. I don't mind when that happens, for it prolongs the anticipation. Once I have succeeded, I open the top, as though to reassure myself that nothing has magically appeared there, as the chest itself seemed to have been a gift to me, wrought for my own specific purpose.

After looking into the emptiness, I remove the bottom, revealing that color so difficult to capture. I lift out the shell, and run my hand over the back, the ridges so slight that it still feels smooth. I turn the shell over and peer into it, my eyes following the spiral on the edge.

On days when I am very brave, I hold the opening of the shell to my ear to hear the waves, and I am with Jacob's bones at the bottom of the sea.

Rebecca D'Harlingue writes about seventeenth-century women taking a different path. Her debut novel, *The Lines Between Us,* is about a young woman who flees Madrid, and the woman who discovers why, three centuries later. Her second novel, *The Map Colorist*, is due out in September 2023 from She Writes Press. It is set in Amsterdam in 1660, and features a younger Anneke, who also appears in her short story, "The Shell." Learn more about D'Harlingue at www.rebeccadharlingue.com and follow her on Facebook, Instagram, and BookBub.

JOANNA'S CHOICE
BY C.V. LEE

SEPTEMBER 1496, ISLE OF JERSEY

Joanna paused from her work to watch the ships bobbing in St. Aubin's Bay. With sails furled, their masts looked like a copse of trees that had shed its leaves. How fitting, given the season. She resumed laying out her wares on a table made from a couple of wooden crates and a board. Soon the ships' crews would flood the marketplace, eager to spend their earnings.

This was her first day selling alone, with no John or Jane beside her in the stall. *Lord, how she missed her children.* She folded and refolded the blankets to best display the spray of purple orchids she had lovingly embroidered on the corner of each. Although blankets were a basic necessity, she believed they could be a thing of beauty, providing a bit of cheer during the dark days of winter.

Satisfied with her efforts, she moved onto the baskets of socks. As she arranged them for the third time, a damsel, clad in a rose-colored gown, her blond hair cascading down her back, approached.

"Good morning," Joanna said in her most cheerful voice.

The damsel smiled and ran her fingers across the top blanket. It warmed Joanna's heart when patrons appreciated the little embellishment she added.

The damsel reached for her coin purse. "How much?"

"Fifteen shillings," Joanna replied.

The damsel squared her shoulders. "You are delusional if you believe anyone would pay such an exorbitant price for these inferior woolens."

"If you seek a bargain," Joanna replied, "it is better to wait until the end of the day. But with so many ships in the harbor, it is not a good day to haggle."

The young woman's cheeks colored. "I do not need advice from the likes of you."

"One last thing: you will have more success if you refrain from insulting the merchant."

The damsel whirled about and stalked away, the hem of her gown dragging carelessly through the dirt as she disappeared into the sea of brightly colored booths.

Joanna shivered, unsure whether from the nip in the autumn air or the damsel's chilly demeanor. She glanced over at Maggie in the next booth. Maggie, with her gray headscarf and plump rosy cheeks, rolled her eyes and shrugged. No one would dare be so bold with a man. But Joanna had little time to fret over the unfairness of it as the crowd surged into St. Helier's Square like an incoming tide.

Proprietors shouted above the din of bleating sheep, clucking chickens, and the musical strains of the wandering troubadours. Patrons called out greetings to their friends as they milled about, filling their baskets with freshly harvested apples, dried eels, and earthen pots; exclaiming over the beauty of the damasks and silks from the east.

Seamen and locals lined up to purchase Joanna's thick woolen socks and soft fleece blankets. As the sun climbed in the sky and the temperature soared, she was grateful for the cover of the booth, giving her moments of shade as she scurried to keep up the hectic pace. The work was nearly as tiring as chasing after the Seigneur of St. Ouen's children, but the extra monies helped support her elderly father.

When the bells of St. Helier's Church rang noon, the crowd thinned as folks pushed their way into local taverns and inns for dinner. She wiped her brow with her apron and, taking advantage of the lull, stepped out from behind the table to tidy the yet unsold items.

"Pardon." A baritone voice startled her. She turned and locked eyes with a stranger standing a few feet away. He touched the rolled brim of his hat in greeting. "I wish to purchase a blanket and three pairs of socks. What kind of bargain can you offer?"

Joanna skirted the table, putting it between her and the seaman before responding. From his accent, she discerned he was a foreigner, most likely hailing from Flanders or Holland. And a man of some means, given the superior cut of his green tunic and the quality of the dagger tucked in his girdle. "My woolens are of the finest quality and in high demand. The only price I am willing to negotiate will be an increase."

"You must think me daft!" His smile bespoke amusement. "Why would I pay more?"

Meeting his eye, Joanna replied, "To have the satisfaction of knowing you have performed a good deed."

He raised a brow. "How so?"

"I bestow the difference to feed the poor. Or, if you prefer, I can set aside a pair of socks or a warm blanket for a needy child."

The seaman dug into his pouch and withdrew several coins. "I admire your care for the less fortunate." He placed the money on the table. "This should suffice to pay for my purchase, as well as socks and a blanket for two urchins."

"I promise two deserving lads will benefit from your charity." Joanna counted the coins and handed two back.

The man lifted his hand. "Keep it and help another child. It has been a profitable year. No one deserves to be cold, especially not a blameless child."

"Bless you—"

"The name is Hendrik."

"I am Joanna. Pleased to make your acquaintance." She wrapped his purchases and handed the package to him. "God bless you, Hendrik, for your generosity."

Joanna watched as he walked away, the package tucked beneath his arm. If only more people were as caring about the poor among them.

A cabbage hurtled through the air, barely missing her head, and landed in her booth. A male voice shouted, "Hedge-born whore!"

Her hands balled into fists as she scanned the square for the offender. A group of damsels glanced her way and giggled. Joanna recognized the young woman in the rose-colored gown from earlier. A tall young man with dark, shoulder-length hair and a short blue tunic approached the group, and the girl in the rose-colored gown placed a coin in his palm.

Joanna curbed her instinct to yell at the youths. She had learned long ago that giving into the impulse of anger always hurt her more than keeping silent; partly from her own guilt at behaving in such an unladylike and unchristian manner, but also the loud whispers afterward, disparaging her character. She was grateful Maggie had not witnessed the scene, for Maggie would have given them a scolding. Joanna did not care to bring more attention to herself.

She closed her eyes and took a couple of deep breaths. At thirty-three, the insults still stung. She should be used to it by now. Living on a small island, there was no place to hide from one's past. Those damsels were too young to remember the stories that spread like a wildfire upon her return to Jersey. All might have been forgotten but for the old crones who jawed over every juicy morsel of gossip, like sheep chewing their cud, vomiting up the vile rumors year after year, passing them down to each new generation, never letting them die.

Opening her eyes, they locked with those of Hendrik, who stood a short way off. She quickly glanced away, stooping down to clean up the mess of cabbage leaves. *Of all the people to have witnessed what had happened.* After putting the pieces in an empty crate, she set about reorganizing her stock, setting aside three blankets and three pairs of socks for children back in St. Ouen's parish.

Three young men, including the tall youth who had received the coin, strutted toward her booth. They could not be more than fifteen, feigning themselves swains, despite being nothing more than lowly peasants known for their fondness for mischief. She drew in a sharp breath as they approached, but they turned and sauntered past. Slowly, she released the air from her lungs, only to gasp and shrink back when they whirled about and rushed into the stall. Two flipped over the baskets, leaving the socks strewn in the dirt. The tall one shoved past her and tipped over the table, spilling the blankets onto the ground.

Joanna placed her hands on her hips and spoke sternly, as

she would to the children in the nursery when they misbehaved. "Pick them up," she demanded, "or I will tell your parents."

The tall one, the apparent ringleader, leered at her. "Your threats do not scare me." He dug into his pouch and held up a shilling. "We are just looking for a bit of fun." He grabbed her wrist and pulled. "There is a hedge over there."

She broke his grip and rubbed her wrist. "There is nothing for sale here but socks and blankets."

"I have heard otherwise," the ringleader sneered.

Maggie stalked into the booth, wagging her finger at the boys. "Get out, ye witless knaves."

The young men laughed as they moved on. "We shall be waiting for you along the road," the tallest one yelled over his shoulder.

Her muscles trembled as much from anger as from fear. How she wished John were here. His very presence had deterred the heckling and lewd propositions. Or even Jane. There was safety in numbers. But she didn't fault either of them for choosing to move to London.

Maggie wrapped an arm around her shoulders. "Pay them no mind. They just like to make trouble."

Joanna nodded. Dropping to her knees, she righted the first basket and began picking up the socks. She felt a presence next to her and, thinking it was Maggie, she said, "I am glad you are here. You have always been a good friend."

"May I help?" Her head jerked up as she recognized the baritone voice. Hendrik squatted down beside her, his blue eyes soft with compassion.

Her eyes searched out Maggie, who grinned. "I know when my help is unwelcome."

"Please stay," Joanna pleaded.

Maggie winked and hastened to her booth. "I have a customer to attend."

Joanna busied herself with retrieving the merchandise. She would admonish Maggie later. The woman knew her wariness of strange men. Reaching for a pair of socks, her hand met Hendrik's. Her fingers closed around the socks. She peered up at him through lowered lashes, noticing for the first time how handsome he looked, with his tanned skin and blond curls tumbling about his shoulders. "I can do this myself."

"It would be my pleasure to help," he replied.

She snatched her hand back and dropped the socks into the basket. "I will not lie with you."

A pained look crossed his face. "I would never deign to expect such a thing from a lady."

Joanna's heart pounded. "Please, pardon my outburst. You do not deserve to be the target of my ire. I know you heard those boys, and I assumed—"

"Already forgiven." Hendrik picked up another pair of socks and dropped them into the basket. "Where is your brother? A lady should not be unaccompanied."

Her hands felt damp. Rising, she wiped them on her apron. "I don't have a brother."

Hendrik picked up a blanket, brushed away the dirt, and folded it. "I have passed your stall before and noticed a man with your same distinctive eyes."

"You speak of my son."

"You are married?"

Her breathing quickened, and she looked away, scolding herself for divulging more information than was wise, choosing not to answer.

He rose and handed her the blanket. "Widowed?"

She snatched it from him, more roughly than necessary. Her

mother would have reprimanded her for her rudeness, but this was about protecting herself. If she showed her prickly side, he might move along. "I prefer not to discuss my life with strangers. If you please, I prefer to finish on my own."

"My apologies. I meant no offense." When Joanna did not respond, Hendrick bowed. "As you wish." He spun around and walked away without a backward glance.

Joanna reassembled the makeshift table, then unfolded and refolded the blankets, unable to shrug off her remorse at treating him abominably when he had been nothing but kind. She tried to justify her conduct by reminding herself that if he knew the truth, his courtesy would have been replaced by contempt.

The afternoon passed swiftly. When the bells of St. Helier's Church rang three times, marking the end of the market, the crowd dispersed.

She gathered the items she had set aside into one basket and hefted it onto her shoulder. She carried it across the square to where she had left her cart that morning and loaded it into the bed. Returning to the booth, she breathed a prayer of thankfulness she had so little merchandise to haul home.

She broke down the table, and once the pieces were tucked away in the cart, she returned to dismantle the booth. She grappled with the poles. At times like this, she realized how much she had depended on John and Jane. Unfortunately, Maggie was already gone.

When the last pole came loose, the canvas dropped over her head. Darkness enveloped her, and a cry escaped her lips. Her breathing grew rapid as she wrestled with the cloth, pulling it one way and then the other, until it finally dropped to the ground. She closed her eyes, trying to steady her nerves. After all these years, she still had not conquered her fear of the dark.

Her body trembled as she folded the canvas and wrapped it around the poles.

As she lugged the awkward bundle through the now nearly empty square, she heard the crunch of leaves behind her. She glanced over her shoulder and saw Hendrik approaching. "May I help?"

Joanna continued walking. "No, I can handle it on my own."

"Tell me you have someone accompanying you home," he said.

They reached the cart, and Joanna heaved the bundle into the bed. "I do not need anyone to take care of me."

Hendrik placed his hand on the side of the cart. "I am just concerned. I heard that dastard's threat."

She waved her hand. "Idle talk. A popinjay trying to prove his manhood."

"It is more than that." Hendrik frowned. "I overheard them making plans. Please, allow me to see you home safely."

"And let you risk your ship leaving without you? I think not."

"My ship will wait."

"Why are you being so kind?"

"I could never forgive myself if I heard that something happened to you and I had done nothing to stop it."

She swallowed hard, abashed by his kindness after her own rudeness. "I accept your offer, and please accept my apologies for my behavior earlier."

He gave a quick nod. "Forgotten like it never happened. Now, do you have a horse to pull this rig?"

"My ass is in the field across the way." She hastened away, thankful for a moment to reflect on what had just occurred. She must be mad, giving that man permission to walk the six miles home with her. He seemed an upstanding sort, but dishonorable intentions ofttimes hid behind a mask of attentiveness.

The ass brayed and kicked the dirt as she came up behind it. "It is just me, Mathilda." She patted the animal's nose to calm it. Joanna's hands trembled as she untied the rope wrapped around a large alder tree and led the animal back to the cart where Hendrik waited.

He put out his hand. "Let me harness the beast."

She handed him the rope, relieved to not have to complete such a task under his scrutiny. "Her name is Mathilda."

The ass stubbornly refused to move, and it took several minutes to get her into the yoke. Joanna marveled that a man of his profession refrained from yelling or cursing at the headstrong creature.

When he finished, he asked, "Which way?"

Joanna gulped, reminding herself she should be grateful. He had given her no reason to suspect his intentions. "West. I live on the far side of the island."

Hendrik walked alongside Joanna, leading Mathilda. Several times their progress was slowed as they moved off the road to allow members of the gentry, astride their horses, to pass.

The traffic lessened, and Joanna took Mathilda's rope as they traveled out of town into the countryside. On either side of the lane, newly harvested fields smelled of cut wheat and rye and freshly turned soil. About a mile out of town, they turned westward onto a tree-lined lane. Behind the line of oak trees, low fences surrounded the stone cottages.

"I have never explored beyond St. Helier," Hendrik said. "I never knew the island was so quaint."

"The north and south sides of the island are quite different," Joanna replied. "No doubt you have observed the rocky cliffs of the north when you have sailed past."

"I have." Hendrik kicked aside a rock in the road. "I get the impression that you, like this island, have a different side as well."

"How so?"

"I perceive you are a lady, yet you pretend otherwise. Perchance you are down on your luck. Or maybe you just like to make sport."

A leaf floated down onto the roadway, startling Mathilda. Joanna made noises, trying to calm the beast before she responded to Hendrik. "Sorry to disappoint, but I am just plain Joanna, a peasant girl from St. Ouen's parish."

"Surely you jest!" Hendrik cocked his head to the side. "Your manners betray you."

"My mother insisted the circumstances of my birth need not prevent me from acquitting myself like a daughter of the gentry."

Hendrik grinned. "I think I should like your mother. Will you do me the honor of introducing us?"

"I fear that is not possible." The conversation was becoming too personal. Joanna quickened her step, trying to stay ahead of Hendrik, hoping to limit the conversation to only necessary subjects like directions.

At that moment, Mathilda halted. Joanna grabbed a handful of oats from the cart and sprinkled them along the path. But no matter how much she tried to trick the animal, the ass refused to move.

Hendrik sidled up to the other side of Mathilda and held out his hand. "Let me try."

Joanna handed him the rope and moved to the side of the

lane. A smile tugged at her mouth, knowing she was about to be entertained.

Hendrik tugged the rope, whispering words of encouragement, but the animal only put her ears back and brayed loudly in protest, digging in her hooves. Joanna giggled at the picture they made, and Hendrik joined in, laughing heartily.

She knelt beneath an oak tree and pushed away the fallen leaves before settling down and spreading out her gray skirt. "Sit and rest a bit. She is stubborn and will not move until she is ready."

Dropping the rope, Hendrik walked over to the tree. "A ship is the same. I have been stranded for days in the middle of the sea, waiting for a wind." Hendrik sat on the ground a few feet away, stretching out his long legs. "This will give us a chance to know each other better."

Joanna steered the conversation away from herself. "We were lucky to have such fine weather this year. Last year, early rains destroyed some of the crops."

"So, do you help with the reaping?" he asked. "I had taken you for a spinster."

"I am a nursery maid and spin when I have time." She plucked a wildflower near the base of the tree and breathed in the scent. "Why did you become a seaman?"

"I followed in my father's footsteps. Like him, I love the salt air and the thrill of the open sea. But my family hails from Utrecht."

"City life does not hold your interest?" It surprised Joanna how comfortable she felt around this stranger.

"I am an adventurer. There is so much to see and learn in this world to stay in only one place."

"What of your family? Your wife and children must miss you dreadfully when you are gone."

Hendrik shook his head. "There is no one. I have never been inclined to marry, and my mother and father died of the plague several years ago."

She reached out her hand and touched his arm. "I am sorry. I pray you find comfort. My mother went home to God last year." Tears pricked the back of her eyes. The year had been hard without her mother, and with her children recently gone to London, her heart felt even more empty.

He placed a hand over hers. "I wish you comfort in return, but do not pity me." He smiled at her, but there was a tinge of sadness in his blue eyes. "I have explored many exciting lands. I have climbed the mountains of Castile, marveled at the art and architecture in Naples, ridden a camel in the Moroccan desert, and browsed the Moorish marketplace with its gold baubles and ivory carvings."

Joanna pulled her hand away and gazed at him in wonder. As a peasant, she was bound to her lord, the Seigneur of St. Ouen. Even if she were a freewoman, she would never have enough money to travel the world. "I envy you, for I have only been to London."

"How does a peasant girl come to visit London? You are a mystery I am curious to solve."

At that moment, Mathilda moved off down the roadway, and Joanna scrambled up from the grass and ran to catch up. When she reached the ass, she grabbed the rope and patted her neck. "Good girl," she whispered, thankful the animal had saved her from needing to answer Hendrik's question. She heard Hendrik's footfalls as he ran to catch up.

The silence was awkward as Hendrik awaited her response. Instead, she asked, "Have you ever attended the St. Lawrence Day faire?"

"I have not."

"It is a riotous event, sure to please a seaman."

"Sounds diverting, but that hardly answers my question. Perchance it amuses you to trifle with me."

Never did she want to see those gentle eyes look at her with abhorrence. Pasting a smile on her face, Joanna replied, "I should hate to lose your good opinion."

Hendrik grinned. "Try me."

"As you wish," Joanna said. "My mother was born in England, a daughter of the gentry. When King Edward came to the throne, she fled with her father to Jersey and married a lowly groom."

"That explains much," Hendrick said. "Tell me of your children."

"I have two, a son and a daughter. They are grown and moved to London about a fortnight ago."

"If indeed you are bound to the Seigneur of St. Ouen, how came your children to be free?"

"The seigneur owed me a favor, and I begged their freedom." While their departure brought her sorrow, she was grateful that they could escape the shame of their past. Her past.

"And what of your husband?"

Joanna struggled to find the words; an answer that veiled the truth, but was not really a lie.

Ahead, a bush swayed and the three young men from the market stepped out from the shadows. The ringleader looked Hendrik up and down, and a cruel sneer crossed his face. "Seems the whore still has a taste for a seaman's prick."

Hendrik stepped in front of Joanna. "I suggest you move along."

They laughed and encircled Hendrik and Joanna. "No need

to be selfish," the leader replied. "We can all take our turn. Fie, I shall even let you watch."

"Sorry to disappoint, but the lady is going home."

"Lady!" the leader spat in the dirt as the other boys laughed. "Is that what she told you? I fear she has deceived you, old man. She is nothing more than a harlot."

Hendrik fondled the hilt of the dagger tucked in his girdle. "I suggest you leave before you regret it."

The ringleader jeered. "He means to fight for the whore's honor."

Drawing the dagger from its sheath, Hendrik grabbed the ringleader's wrist and quickly twisted his arm behind him, holding the dagger to his throat. The ringleader gasped in pain as Hendrik pulled his arm higher. Still defiant, the ringleader sneered, "If you think you can take on all three of us, you are wrong."

The two other boys moved closer.

"Are you sure you want to try me?" Hendrik turned his dagger toward the other two, slashing it downward and cutting the sleeve of the closest one's tunic. "I have fended off many a pirate."

The two raised their hands to their chests and took a step backward. "We are not looking for trouble." Turning, they hopped the low fence and raced across the field.

Hendrik released the ringleader. "Away with you, filthy scum."

The ringleader spat on Hendrik's boots. "Make her earn every penny." He pivoted on his heel and ran to catch up to his friends.

Hendrik watched as they scampered across the field, weaving to avoid the cows. Glancing toward Joanna, he asked. "Are you well?"

She shook her head. Her stomach churned at the dour look on Hendrik's face. She wandered to the side of the roadway and leaned against a tree. "Give me a moment."

"It is not safe for a woman to travel alone. I am surprised your husband—"

Joanna felt her ire rise. "I will not discuss this with you." She pushed away from the tree and hurried to catch up with Mathilda, who, realizing they were close to home, continued down the road unattended.

They journeyed on in silence. The road curved, and the trees thinned, revealing gently sloping hills and flocks of sheep being herded in for the night. They crested the hill as the sun sank low over St. Ouen's Bay. Gulls soared above the water, and the heavens splayed with the colors of pink, orange, and lavender against the darkening sky.

Joanna broke the silence. "I appreciate your rescuing me. My father's cottage is down the hill. There is no need for you to go any further."

"Do you need help unloading the cart?"

"I am quite capable of doing it myself."

Hendrik inclined his head. "It is a bit late to return to St. Helier tonight. Is there an inn nearby where I might find a bed?"

She pointed to a path heading northeast. "The manor is down the road. The seigneur and his wife always have an open door. You are welcome to dine and stay there for the night."

She watched until Hendrik disappeared around the bend in the road, feeling a touch of sadness. He seemed a nice man, and their conversation was pleasant. If only things were different. If only her past did not cast a shadow over her future, she would have confided she had no husband. But there was no point in wasting time regretting things that could never be. Besides, he would be gone in the morning.

Joanna followed Mathilda down the hillside. Unharnessing the animal, she led it into the fenced garden and latched the gate. Returning to the cart, she lifted out the baskets.

The door to the cottage stood ajar, and the aroma of fish stew wafted out. Joanna placed the baskets on the floor beside the door. The last of the setting sun was visible through the open window that looked out on St. Ouen's Bay. This was the time of day when every cobweb in the one-room cottage was visible. The furnishings were decrepit, albeit tidy and in their place, and her father had scattered fresh-cut rushes over the dirt floor.

The breeze picked up. The hinges creaked as the shutters banged against the outer wall. She shivered. Most days, she lived in the luxurious manor house where the rooms were warm at night and the food was plentiful, albeit much noisier with the seigneur's children running about.

Her father sat with his gray head bowed over a bowl of stew. He reached into the basket in the center of the table and took a slice of bread.

"Good e'en, Father."

He lifted his head. "Was that a man with you?" His voice held an accusatory tone, but the twinkle in his amber eyes told her he was teasing.

She smiled. "Were you spying on me again?"

"I was worried by the lateness of the hour. I waited for you at the door, but your attention was so taken by that man, you did not even notice your poor old father."

"He is just a man from the market." She crossed to the window and closed the shutters. "You will catch your death of cold with the evening breeze blowing through the cottage."

"Does this man have a name?"

Joanna picked up a bowl from the low table beneath the window and moved over to stir the kettle that hung over the open fire in the center of the room. She breathed in the aroma of cabbage, leeks, and fish before ladling out a healthy portion.

She settled into the chair next to her father. "Hendrik. He is a seaman who hails from Utrecht."

"And what is your opinion of this Hendrik fellow?"

Dipping her spoon in the stew, she raised it to her lips and blew to cool it. "He appears amiable and well-spoken. It was most thoughtful of him to accompany me home. I pray he will not find his ship has sailed by the time he gets back to St. Helier."

Her father laughed. "You need not worry about Hendrik."

"You know him?" She gaped, but quickly recovered. "Surely you jest."

"I would not tease about my daughter's suitor." His spoon scraped the bottom of the bowl as he tried to scoop up the last of his stew. "I am pleased he is paying you his attentions."

"How can you be certain it is the same man?"

"I recognized his tall stature and blond curls." With the bread, he sopped up the last of the gravy. "If he makes you an offer, I hope you will accept."

"He is hardly a suitor. I doubt I shall ever see him again. Besides, how could I leave you? If I am not here, who will care for you?"

"I can care for myself." James snatched up his napkin and dabbed at the gravy on his chin. "You need not sacrifice your chance at happiness on my account."

For the first time in a long while, she felt shy before this man who had raised her and loved her. "Really, Father. No one is discussing marriage. And even if he were, it is not likely he could pay the bride price."

He placed a hand on her arm. "Do not be so certain. I would die a happy man knowing you were cared for."

Digging through her apron, Joanna pulled out a kerchief and finished wiping the gravy from his face. "Only for you would I consider it." He beamed, and Joanna flicked the kerchief, hitting his arm. "Now, put those foolish thoughts out of your head."

She rose and picked up the dirty bowls and spoons. Leaning down, she kissed his cheek. How she wished he was truly her father.

THE MURMUR of voices and the clatter of moving furniture awakened Hendrik. For a moment, he was unsure of where he was. But the snoring and the smell of unwashed bodies reminded him he was in the great hall at St. Ouen's Manor. His bones felt weary. It had been a long time since he'd slept on the floor alongside the peasants.

He scrambled up from the floor and strapped on his sword, tucking his dagger into his girdle. After rolling up the sleeping mat, a servant showed him where to stow it.

Candles flickered, causing shadows to dance on the dark paneled walls. Hendrik's boots clomped on the planked floor as he crossed to the sideboard on the opposite wall. Grabbing a trencher, he filled it with a large portion of salmon, fruit, cheese, and bread before settling onto a bench at one of the many trestle tables. A page placed a tankard of ale in front of him. He drank deeply, then tackled his food, surprised by how hungry he was.

He had meant to speak with the Seigneur of St. Ouen last night, but Philippe and his lady had taken to bed early. He did not regret accompanying Joanna home yesterday. Quite the contrary, for he had never met a woman like her, so independent, pleasant to converse with, and possessing a head for business. With her blond curls and trim figure, she had been pleasing on the eyes, as well. However, his chivalry had left him in a predicament. He needed to get back to St. Helier before his ship was due to sail at noon. Indeed, he should be there to oversee the loading of his vessel. Hopefully, his past business dealings with the seigneur would be enough to secure him a right good steed for the journey back.

Now, he intended to address the seigneur regarding an unexpected matter of personal business. Over supper last night, he had made a few inquiries and, to his delight, discovered Joanna had no husband. He smiled as he spooned in a mouthful of fish. Yesterday, he had stepped off the boat, content with his bachelor status. But after a night's sleep, he was convinced that Joanna possessed all the qualities he desired in a wife. What a surprise for his crew should he return to his ship a married man!

Footsteps sounded behind him and a raspy male voice said, "Captain Hendrik, to what do I owe the pleasure?"

He turned and stared. Philippe's face was gaunt, his shoulders stooped, his hair thinned and completely gray. Hendrik had heard rumors about the seigneur's detention in the dungeon at Mont Orgueil. The confinement had aged Philippe at least a score since they last met.

Recovering from the shock, he stood and bowed. "Seigneur de Carteret. I am pleased to see you again. I find myself here as I accompanied a lady home from the market yesterday. She claims to be one of your peasants."

Philippe gave him a questioning look. "That was kind of you."

"However, I find myself in a bind. I must return to St. Helier immediately. Pray, could you spare me a horse for the journey and a moment of your time to speak privily?"

"Certainly," Philippe replied. "I have a few minutes before mass."

Hendrik followed Philippe to his study. Dark, engraved wood covered the walls, and a fire blazed on the hearth. Hendrik wandered over to study the painting of a black horse that hung on the wall behind the desk.

"My father's beloved destrier." Philippe shut the door and settled into the chair behind the desk. "Quite the tale if we had the time." He pointed to the seat opposite. "What did you wish to discuss?"

Hendrik settled into the intricately carved wooden chair. "A lady named Joanna."

"I take it she is the peasant you accompanied home. Is there a problem?"

Hendrik shifted in the chair, trying to get comfortable. "I wish to marry her."

Philippe frowned. "Are there not plenty of maidens in Utrecht for you to choose from? Given the size of your holdings, I would think even a nobleman would not object to you marrying his daughter."

Hendrik met Philippe's eyes. "None has caught my fancy. I have no desire to spend my days listening to the latest gossip of the gentry. Yet, the daughters of freemen lack the social graces."

"By your standards, I doubt Joanna would measure up. She is neither gentry nor free born."

Hendrik wiped the moisture from his forehead. The room was warm, and he had not expected an interrogation. "I find Joanna meets my requirements perfectly."

Philippe furrowed his brow. "And you know this after so short an acquaintance?"

"I require a wife who can handle my business affairs while I am at sea. Joanna comports herself like a lady, and I shan't complain about having a woman to warm my bed at night. I am willing to pay a handsome bride price."

"If I did not know you to be such an upstanding man, I would refuse outright. Have you spoken of this to Joanna?"

"Of course not. I would not wish to get her hopes up. Besides, I have not the luxury of time for a courtship. Hence, I beseech your permission to take her as my wife forthwith."

Philippe coughed, his chest rattling. "I am loath to part with her. A good nursemaid is difficult to find."

"How many years until her services are no longer required, and she be left to grow old alone in that cottage by the sea? With me, she would want for nothing. Name your price."

"I would never force her hand."

"Your resistance confuses me." Hendrik paused for a moment, unsure if he would be pressing a matter that was better left alone. He leaned back in the chair, wondering where the answer to his next question might lead. "Perchance she is your paramour?"

"Certainly not. You would have to search far and wide to find a marriage more successful than my own. Lady Margaret and I are blissfully happy on both sides of the chamber door. Joanna is my goddaughter and has suffered grievously at the hands of men."

"How so?"

"You need to ask her, for it is not my tale to tell." Philippe rose and shuffled over to the window and stared out. "A word of caution. If I were to grant my blessing, and she were to agree, do not expect a marriage in every sense of the word."

"But she would be my wife." The mystery of Joanna was becoming more puzzling.

"If you demand submission from a woman, you change who she is. Besides, the marriage bed is a happier place with a willing partner."

Hendrik nodded and lapsed into silence for several minutes, then dug into his pouch and pulled out a bag of coins and dropped them on the table. "I shall accept whatever terms she demands. That should be sufficient funds to purchase her freedom." Hendrik stood and moved to the door. "I return to Jersey in a fortnight. I trust you can convince her to accept my offer. But should she refuse, pray, give her the money."

"I fear you esteem too highly my powers of persuasion." Philippe limped across the room and opened the door. "Now, I must hurry or I shall miss mass. Godspeed, Captain Hendrik."

When Philippe was gone, Hendrik rose and went in search of the stable. His mind was uneasy, as neither Joanna nor Philippe seemed willing to divulge even a whit of her past, other than a man had misused her. Or did he say men? As he strode down the path, the voice branding her a hedge-born whore echoed in his brain, along with the picture of that reprobate accusing her of preferring a seaman's prick.

He had assumed they were cruel words for a handsome woman who would not submit to their overtures. Yet, the accusation was so precise it evoked a suspicion there may be truth behind the words.

JOANNA'S CHOICE

WITH THE CHILDREN behaving so unruly, the week passed like a blur for Joanna. The boys refused to be diverted from tormenting their sister, Maybelle. At two, the babe was no easy child, believing herself capable of doing anything her brothers could. By nightfall, Joanna fell into bed so weary she barely had time to think before drifting off to sleep.

Saturday proved especially rough, as the boys placed lizards in Maybelle's bed. Maybelle had made such a to-do it seemed everyone in the house had descended on the nursery to discern the cause of the commotion.

As evening approached, Joanna resorted to bribing the boys with an extra piece of apple cake to get them to vespers on time. During the service, the priest glared at the children several times as they refused to stop whispering, no doubt planning more mischief.

A vision of Hendrik popped into her head. How pleasant it had been to have an adult conversation. She loved the de Carteret children dearly, but tonight, she wondered if her acceptance of so many years of chaos and absurd logic had just been a way to escape facing the real world.

After evensong, Philippe waved her over. "I need to speak with you."

In silence, they walked from the chapel to the manor house. Trembling, she ascended the two steps and followed him through the large double doors. The light from the fire cast shadows on the dark, wood-paneled walls. The clomp of his boots as they crossed the great hall to his study added an air of foreboding. Surely, he would not dismiss her after all these years.

Philippe opened the door and motioned for her to enter.

The heat from the fire felt oppressive even before she stepped inside. He shuffled over and stood with his back to the hearth. In the dim light, he looked more like his former self, the man who had found her on the streets of London. Back then, he had made a dashing figure astride his white horse.

Philippe gestured toward the high-backed wooden chair beside the fire. She sat, hands primly folded, waiting for her rebuke for failing to keep the children under control.

"I wish to discuss Captain Hendrik."

Joanna fumbled with her rosary until she found the cross and gripped it in her palm. "I hardly know the man."

"He has asked to marry you, and I have given him my blessing."

Inwardly, Joanna raged, even as she struggled to keep her outward countenance calm. How unfair that two men could conspire to turn her life upside down, determining her future without her consent. "I do not wish to marry."

Philippe raked his fingers through his hair. "He has already paid the bride price."

Every part of her body felt hot and sticky, and she wiped her palms on her skirt. All she was to these men was a piece of property to be bought and sold, no different from the blankets she sold at the market. As her godfather, and the one person who knew the most about her ordeal, she had thought that at least he would have considered her a human being with desires and feelings. And yet, as soon as someone dropped a filled purse in front of him, he had sold her without hesitation.

Philippe knelt down before her and took her hands in his. "I would never have agreed if I did not believe this was for the best."

She wished to pull her hands away. "Is this my punishment for failing to keep the children out of trouble?"

Philippe stood and settled into a chair beside her. "I assure you, it is not. I wish to secure your future."

Joanna met his gaze. "You promised to care for me."

He looked away. "I am caring for you. Sadly, I will not live forever, and I fear my time is short."

"Can you not insist Edouard fulfill your promise when he becomes seigneur?"

Philippe dropped his chin to his chest. "I cannot guarantee my son will honor my promise. But I trust Hendrik to care for you."

Joanna's mouth went dry, and she eyed the flagon, wishing for a drink, if only to boost her courage. "Do not make me do this."

"I informed Hendrik the choice is yours."

"Then my answer is no. You must return his money."

"I beg you not to be so hasty in your refusal," Philippe said. "Give it some thought. But should you decide against him, Hendrik has instructed me to give you the money."

It seemed her tongue could find no words to respond to such a thoughtful gesture. Hendrik's gentle eyes and kind manner must be sincere.

Philippe stood and shuffled over to the hearth. He looked so frail. It was still jarring to see the damage his internment had wrought. "Captain Hendrik returns in a sennight and requires a response. Go with my blessing. I wish you happiness."

He turned his back to her, and she knew she had been dismissed. She slipped out the door and dashed up the stairs to fetch her cloak. Despite the darkness, she headed out of the manor and made her way to her father's cottage.

Joanna awoke the next morning still distraught over her conversation with Philippe. Rising from her sleeping mat, she crossed to the other side of the cottage and knelt before the old chest where she stored her spindles. She ran her hand over the carved wood, marveling at the intricate work. With her finger, she traced the flowers, then the shapes along the base that reminded her of cathedral windows.

A hand touched her shoulder. "I miss her, too," her father whispered.

"Mother once told me you made it for her."

"A wedding gift." There was pride in his voice.

Joanna brushed her hand across the heart-shaped lock. "Wherever did you find a clasp like this?"

"At the St. Lawrence faire. A peddler had an old garment chest amongst his wares. Told me he found it in Ireland. It was in such disrepair it wasn't worth a pence. But the lock! It was beautiful, just like my Thomasse."

"Your love for her shines through in every detail."

"We were happy, just as I know you will be happy with Hendrik."

"Seigneur de Carteret told you."

James nodded.

"I cannot do this." Joanna's voice cracked. "He will have expectations."

"Joanna, look at me." She turned and gazed into her father's eyes. He took her hands in his. "It is different when you love someone."

"No one mentioned love."

He pushed back a lock of her hair and let his thumb caress her cheek. "Give it time. I know he will come to love you." He lapsed into silence, and his eyes took on a faraway expression. "Did your mother ever tell you she did not want to marry me? If it had not been for you, she would never have agreed to be my wife. With time, she grew to love me."

"What if one day he hears the rumors? He will feel nothing but disdain. I could not bear that."

"Hendrik is a good man. If you confided in him, I am sure he would understand." Her father stood. "I shall be at the stable."

WHEN THE DOOR closed behind her father, Joanna picked up the chest and placed it on the table. Opening the lid, she withdrew a spindle, distaff, and a handful of fleece. Troublesome decisions were easier to ponder when her hands were busy. Spinning made her feel close to her mother. And right now, she yearned for her comforting advice.

Drafting a bit of fleece from the distaff, she wrapped it around the hook on the end of the spindle. Twisting it, she dropped it and watched as it spun the wool into thread.

As a young maid, she had dreamed of romance and being wed to the one who captured her heart. But that dream turned into a nightmare when she was but ten and three. It lasted for a decade until Philippe found her in London and brought her home to Jersey with her two children, her past shrouded in mystery.

Upon her return, she resumed her duties as a nursemaid at the manor, but the former declarations of love from her suitors now took the form of vulgar propositions. Over the years, the tales of her transgressions grew. How hard she tried to make an outward show of pretending not to care, while inwardly, her heart broke. It came as a relief when Lady Margaret had given her permission to take her meals in the nursery with the younger children.

The spindle stopped. She inspected the thread quality. With the first spindle filled, she opened the chest again and removed an empty one, along with more fleece to wrap around the distaff.

Now she was tasked with a difficult choice. Marrying Hendrik would mean leaving behind everything she loved, everything that was familiar. How could she leave her father, the man who had raised her, loved her, even though she was not his child? For his sacrifice, he deserved to be cared for in his old age.

Even as she dreaded the prospect of wifely duties, it was tempting to escape this place, to live where her past was like a blank page. It would be like the priest had often spoken from the pulpit, her sins washed clean and thrown into the Sea of Forgetfulness. Even if she would never forget.

Yet, life with Hendrik would mean stepping into the unknown. It would be a whole new life, with a new language and new customs. What if she was unhappy? Or Hendrik only dissembled kindness?

By the time the distaff was empty and all the wool spun, she was not one whit closer to a decision.

THE FOLLOWING week passed like a whirlwind, with little time to think. Despite her weariness, Joanna slept little, her mind wrestling with her conflicting emotions.

At times, she bemoaned that as a woman her destiny was out of her hands, that a man could walk into her life and upset her world. At others, her body tingled with excitement at the prospect of fresh adventures. There were even moments of gratitude for, despite the pressure from those around her to submit to the marriage, they had granted her the final decision, a choice denied most women.

Then there were the hours of terror, her body covered in sweat, wanting to scream. Instead, she wept silent tears so as not to wake the children. It was a twofold fear—the prospect of sharing a bed with a man, and the possibility of being turned out of Hendrik's home if he discovered the truth about her past.

When she went to bed on Friday night, her decision was made. She would take the risk and confess all to Hendrik. She drifted into a deep, restful sleep. In her dreams, she felt the loving arms of her mother around her whispering into her hair. "Be not afraid. Everything will turn out as it should."

JOANNA WOKE early and hastened to her father's cottage. She loaded the cart with wares for the Saturday market and hitched up Mathilda. She added a satchel, a gift from Lady Margaret, filled with her few worldly belongings; her spindles, her mother's brush, and one change of clothes.

Her father emerged from the cottage carrying a flask of ale and a portion of bread and cheese and tucked it into a corner of the cart.

Joanna threw her arms around his neck and held on tight. "Father!" Her heart ached with love and her vision blurred. "I may never see you again."

Pulling away, he asked, "So, you have decided to marry Hendrik?"

"Nothing is certain. I am taking your advice and shall tell him all. Perchance he will withdraw his offer. Better he knows now than spend my days worrying he might find out."

"I almost forgot!" Her father hastened back into the cottage and returned carrying the carved chest with the heart lock. "I wish you to have this. It will remind you of your mother and me."

A smile lit her face. "I shall cherish it."

He set it in the cart. "I need to show you something." Opening the lid, he beckoned her to look inside. He pressed one corner, and the bottom sprang free.

When he lifted the board, Joanna gasped. Beneath, lay a pearl necklace and more crowns than she could count.

"If Hendrik is not good to you, there is enough here to pay the fare back to Jersey."

"Where did you get all that money?" she asked.

"It is a wedding gift from Seigneur de Carteret. He means to take good care of his goddaughter."

Joanna laughed, then grew serious. "What if I am robbed along the way to St. Helier?"

"A groom will accompany you to bring back the cart and ass. He awaits just over the hill."

Her father replaced the board and closed the lid. He withdrew a black iron key from his pouch and turned it in the lock before placing it in Joanna's hand. "Keep it safe."

She slipped it into the pocket of her apron and kissed his weathered cheek. "Never forget I love you, Father." She picked up the rope attached to Mathilda's bridle and headed down the path. When she reached the top, she turned back. Her father waved, and she blew him one last kiss, her heart torn between the excitement of a new adventure and the desire to hold her father close and never let him go.

The road to St. Helier seemed long as Joanna fretted over what she would say to Hendrik and the uncertainty of how he would react. Fortunately, the groom preferred to walk in silence.

As they turned east onto the last stretch of road into town, she spotted Hendrik leaning against an oak tree. He made a handsome picture surrounded by the red, yellow, and amber leaves, the ocean breeze ruffling his blond curls. Removing his rolled-brim hat, he stepped forward and bowed. "Good day, Joanna."

Her face heated, her words stuck in her throat.

"I pray you have come to a decision." His eyes were full of hope.

Joanna instructed the groom to lead Mathilda up the road a bit and wait for her. "I want you close enough to hear if I call."

Leaving the marked path, she approached Hendrik, grateful he had waited for her some distance from the market, away from curious eyes and prying ears. "Before I give you my answer, we need to talk." Joanna kneeled down and cleared a spot of leaves and fallen acorns, before settling on the ground in the oak's shade.

Hendrik dropped down beside her, his brow furrowed. "Does this mean—" He bit his bottom lip. "What can I say to convince you to accept my offer?"

"I confess, I have been conflicted. I never talk of my past, but it would be wrong to enter a marriage without confessing it." She smoothed her gray skirt before tucking a stray strand of hair behind her ear. She dropped her voice to a whisper. "You may wish to withdraw your offer."

Hendrik took her hands in his. "Let me be the judge."

Swallowing hard, she launched into her prepared speech. "I know, as my husband, you will have expectations. That frightens me, and I want you to know why." She dropped her eyes. "When I was ten and three, pirates kidnapped me." She heard him gasp. "As a seaman, no doubt you have heard tales. To keep me from jumping overboard, they tied me to a hook in the hull. There I lived in the dark amongst the rats. At night, those miscreants would descend the ladder, stumbling in the dark as they groped their way to my mat, smelling of sweat, piss, and sour ale."

It surprised Joanna how aloof she felt telling her story, as if she were talking about someone else. She stood and spoke with her back to him. "I was young and ignorant, and for a long time did not realize I was with child. I lost the last trace of my pride when I bore my son, John, as the pirates gathered around to watch, laughing and placing bets as to who might be the father. When I grew heavy with Jane, they abandoned us on a wharf in the south of England. Fortunately, a kind gentleman and his wife took pity and offered us a ride to London. I feigned a new widow, lest they deem us unfit company; my son being the bastard child of a pirate and another in my womb."

She waited for Hendrik to say something. The silence stretched, and she forced herself to face him, but he turned his head away. The muscle in his temple flinched, and she sensed him recoiling at her presence.

The pain of her shame felt fresh, confirmation of the mistake she had made in sharing the darkest recesses of her heart. She despaired that she even cared what Hendrik thought. Suddenly, she felt moved to finish her tale. "I gave birth to Jane on the streets of London."

"Stop." Hendrik covered his ears. "It is enough."

A tear slid down Joanna's cheek. "I understand. A man of your stature requires a woman of virtue."

He made no answer. Squaring her shoulders, Joanna dashed her hand across her cheek and hastened to where the groom waited with Mathilda and her cart. When she glanced back, Hendrik had vanished.

Despite the autumn chill, the market was hectic. There was a constant line of patrons at Joanna's booth; exactly what she needed to keep her mind off the heaviness in her heart. Her gaze strayed often to the chest stowed beneath the table and her hand groped the pocket of her apron for the key, just to reassure herself they were still there. Philippe would expect his wedding gift to be returned.

However, the constant demands of customers were not enough to stop her from berating herself for her stupidity. Hendrik had been eager to make her his bride until she revealed her deepest secrets. She had desperately wanted him to accept her despite her past. The prospect of escaping the cruel gossip had made marriage a more palatable choice. But deep down, she had known he would reject her—and he had proven her right.

She shivered as the thought evoked memories of her life in London. There, she had lived on the streets, begging for food to feed her children. Lord, she never wanted to know cold and hunger again.

By the time the bells of St. Helier's Church tolled twelve, Joanna had sold her last blanket and pair of socks—a blessing, for she longed to hurry home, crawl into bed, and nurse her wounded heart.

The crowd ducked into taverns and inns or made their way to the grassy area beneath the tall rock to enjoy their noon meal. She gathered her baskets, preparing for the return trip home. Retrieving the chest from under the table, she left the stall. Her gaze landed on Hendrik, standing a few feet away. She wheeled around and headed in the opposite direction.

"Joanna, wait. I wish to speak with you." His baritone voice grew louder as he caught up to her.

She quickened her step. "To what purpose? Your silence told me everything I needed to know." His hand touched her shoulder, and she flinched. She whirled around, her body trembling. "I confessed what I have told no other, and you walked away."

"So you would not witness my anger. No one should suffer as you did."

"I do not want your pity." Her tone was bitter, and she hastened the rest of the way to the cart and placed the chest in the back corner.

She felt his presence behind her. "You are not your past," Hendrik whispered against her hair. "Today, you are a strong, bonny woman, the perfect helpmate for me."

She caught her breath, unsure she had heard him properly. "You still wish to wed?"

He turned her to face him. "My ship leaves in an hour, and the church is but a short distance away." He dropped to one knee. "Marry me, Joanna."

She could hardly believe it. Despite her disclosure, he still wanted her. He had felt anger on her behalf, even defended her from the young men who sought to harm her. Philippe and her father had vouched for his character. She slowly reached out her hand, though she could scarcely see him through her tears. Taking her hand, he stood and looped it through his arm, and together, they crossed the square to St. Helier's Church.

When they reached the porch of the church, Hendrik dug into his pouch and produced a ring. Taking her hand, he slid it on her finger. "With this ring, I thee wed."

She stared into his blue eyes, marveling at the happiness she saw there. Hendrik reached into his pouch again and withdrew an acorn and placed it in her palm. "May our future hold as much promise as this little seed."

He untied another larger pouch which hung from his girdle. From it, he withdrew handfuls of gold coins and threw them into the air. Joanna laughed as the children and a few adults scrambled along the ground to pick them up.

"Now, my dear wife, we must make haste before my crew lifts anchor."

"Let me retrieve my things," Joanna replied, dashing off toward the cart, Hendrik's heavy footsteps sounding close behind her.

Joanna lifted the satchel out of the cart, which Hendrik took from her, and slipped the strap over his head before lifting out the chest. She could get used to having a man help and protect her.

Placing her hand in the crook of his arm, they walked toward the harbor. The warm sun smiled on them as the brilliantly colored leaves danced in the square. As they passed, people clapped and Maggie called out her good wishes. Joanna smiled and waved, scarcely feeling the ground beneath her feet.

They walked up the plank onto the ship's deck. She followed Hendrik up to the bridge, where he set the chest down beside the worn wooden helm. He yelled to his seamen to unfurl the sails and haul up the anchor.

Joanna stood beside her new husband, holding fast to the rail as the ship drifted away from the wharf and out of the harbor into the sea, the Isle of Jersey shrinking until it was nothing more than a tiny speck sinking into the sea.

C.V. Lee brings to life forgotten heroes and heroines of the past. Her Roses & Rebels series is set on the Isle of Jersey during the Late Medieval, Renaissance, and Reformation time periods. The first book in the series is slated for publication in late 2022 or early 2023. For more about C.V. Lee, visit her website at cvlee.com or follow her on Facebook, Instagram, Twitter, or Bookbub for updates on publication dates.

THE DRAGON LORD - A WINTER SOLSTICE TALE

BY ANNE M. BEGGS

CONNACHT, IRELAND, DECEMBER 13, 1225

Eloise stirred to the baby kicking in her womb. Laying her hands upon her swollen belly, she gloried in the miracle of their son growing strong and healthy. Of course, her father, Lord Hubert of Dahlquin, and her husband, Lord Roland of Ashbury At-March, wanted a male heir. Was it wishful thinking she carried a son? It was not. She couldn't explain it; she just knew he was he.

At this early hour, the chamber was cloaked in darkness. Today was Winter Solstice, the shortest day of the year. They would celebrate the mythical battle between the Holly King, winter's dark, and the Oak King, summer's light, with songs, stories, and a dance around the festive bonfire.

Yesterday, Roland had returned from a week at Ashbury At-March. But this cold, dark morning she was in a warm bed, festooned with woolen quilts and a grand, weighty bear fur upon her, nestled against the most magnificent husband any lady could wish for. Come spring, they would have a fine son. She had much to be grateful for and recited a blessing for God and Goddess before taking Roland's hand and placing it on her belly.

He caressed her bulge, but now the baby was still. He moved his hand toward her breast, but she stayed him a moment longer, hoping he would experience the movement within.

"Your son says Good Solstice upon you, Father."

"I hear nothing," Roland murmured, moving his hand back to her breast.

"He was wiggling vigorously," she said, disappointed.

"Good Solstice and me upon you, Dulcinea," he answered, calling her by his private nickname, nuzzling her neck, pressing his erect self against her.

"By your will, let it be so," she said, turning, kissing him. She pushed herself upright. "After I pee."

"Curse it," Roland grumbled, "three months of puking, now all you do is pee."

"And all you do is complain." She squatted over the chamber pot. "Go on, away with you," she said to Fido as the wire-haired hound came to investigate. "Growing a baby is hard work. And it's cold out here."

After wiping herself and her hands on a rag, she pushed the chamber pot back under the bed away from pesky hounds, then crawled back into bed.

"Good Solstice upon me." He pulled her on him.

Early morning hopes were dashed as someone banged on the door.

The dogs rushed to the door; the cats held their ground. Husband and wife waited. Hoping.

"Ellie. Abelard!" Abelard was Hubert's rude nickname for

Roland, reminding him of the perilous punishment the scholar, Peter Abelard, suffered after seducing his student, Heloise.

"Da, what's wrong?" Eloise called, as she and Roland both climbed out of their warm, safe bed to face what problem, quickly finding some nightclothes to cover themselves.

"Your mother, she twisted her ankle. She can't walk," Hubert said, entering the chamber as Roland opened the door.

Roland and Hubert scowled at each other. Both men were tall. Her father was fifty, bald on top with graying light hair, lined blue eyes. Roland was twenty-five, dark complexion, black, wavy hair and brown eyes.

"Always fucking my daughter, when your work is done for a year," Hubert said.

Roland smirked. "Your language."

"Da," Eloise said, wrapping her hands around her belly.

Hubert sniffed then gave Eloise a curt nod. "Grab a robe and come," he said, pointing into the dark towards her garment chest.

"Abelard, get your men up and moving. Her servants too. It's the shortest damned day of the year and we've much to do. And my Lady Aine is hurt."

"Let us go, Da," Eloise said, pushing past him, hounds in tow, anxious to see her injured mother. "By your will, stop calling him Abelard."

"I, too, would like to see our Lady Mother," Roland said, following Eloise, the hounds behind him.

AINE'S FOOT had started to swell. On such a cold morning, heat couldn't be accurately felt. The bruising wouldn't show for a day or two. Eloise sent her mother's servant, Daire—thin, wiry, and as sturdy as the Lady Aine herself—to find some crutches.

"Ellie, pull our garments, will you?" Aine said, pointing to the chest.

Eloise studied her mother's smiling face, sweet green eyes, and her long, blonde hair, still unbraided. How like her mother, strong and attending to the needs of the day, rather than her strained ankle.

Eloise walked to the familiar chest, a wedding gift from Hubert's father, Lord Ruidari, to his son's bride, Aine. The stout wooden chest of oak was tall enough to sit upon, and the flat lid was a handy seat or table. The carvings were extraordinary; on one side was a shield with the English fleur-de-lis, representing sovereignty and protection. On the other was a shield with the Ailm, representing Irish strength. Such a bold political statement from the original Barbarian of Dahlquin. Even more intriguing were the carvings on the front: two ovals, asymmetrical with flower motifs, budding and blooming, and the margins full of flowers. In the center was a large heart, so simple, yet so telling of Eloise's grandfather's, or more specifically, her grandmother's hope that their daughter-in-law would not only be safe and protected but would find love and contentment. The base had symmetrical arched window motifs, fitting for a grand cathedral.

This treasured garment chest held Aine's and Eloise's Solstice garments, and Eloise pulled them from the chest and laid them on the bed: two thick near-white woolen chemises and two near-white surcoats, with pearls and beads sewn on to reflect the firelight and honor the return of the warming, life-giving sun. In summer, a linen chemise complimented the surcoats as the women gave thanks to the sun on the longest day of the growing season.

Eloise held her surcoat up, one hand at her shoulder, the other pressing it to herself, imagining the shimmer of the baubles in the winter firelight. Her long amber hair was still mussed, and hung down her back, as yet unbraided. She gave a small twirl to see the surcoat move.

"How shall we help you dance, *Mathair*? What a glory this night will be. The longest night of the year to spend with Roland." She smiled at him, licking her bottom lip.

Roland met her smile with a glare.

"We have discussed this. You know how I feel about you," Roland paused, "performing."

"Roland, this is Solstice, a celebration to honor the season."

"No," he said in blunt English, as if that would end it.

"You don't—"

"Eloise!" her mother said in sharp reprimand. "You two must speak. *Speak*," she emphasized, glaring at Roland, "in your own chamber. More importantly, listen to each other," Aine said, this time glaring at Eloise.

Eloise looked to her father. Surely, he would explain to Roland the importance of this. The impassive warrior revealed nothing. Her mother tilted her head to the door.

***

Reaching their chamber, Roland held the door open, and Eloise stalked in. The hounds followed him, and he closed the door, but did not bolt it. Dragon retreated to her bed, while Fido and Griffin stood tentatively by. Such disharmony in the pack distressed the loyal beasts.

"I thought I made myself clear. You may not dance before strangers," Roland said, with his raspy voice.

"Strangers? Family. Dahlquin, Connacht, it is our obligation to pay homage to the—"

"Family? My men. A pagan ritual," Roland interrupted.

"Your men *are* family. If they are not, we have a serious problem," she retorted, believing his men were no threat. Her voice turned shrill with offense. "Pagan? God created the heaven and earth, the sun and moon before creating man—"

"No!" He cut her off.

"You don't own me."

He blinked.

"I own every part of you. This is an old argument, why are we still having it?"

"You own what I own."

"Are you denying our marriage contract? Our pledge before God?" Roland narrowed his eyes on her. "The one my brother sought to have annulled. It was important to you then."

"We are husband and wife, and I have given you all I possess, but I disagree with the premise—"

"Disagree with the premise?" Roland croaked. "I own every hair on your body, crown to cleft, every tooth in your head. If I choose to knock them out, I'll still own them," he said clenching his fist as if holding all her teeth therein. "I own your toes, feet, legs and what's between them."

"I own your thoughts and ideas." He paused as if calculating the possibility.

"You can never own my thoughts and ideas." Eloise knew force was not true power. It didn't earn respect or love.

"I own you and what you do. If you commit murder, responsibility is upon me. Everything is on me. Do you understand?"

"If I am condemned as a heretic, it is I who burn, not you. You have great responsibility, but I suffer greater consequences," she said, meeting his sneer.

"Exactly, yet you flit about, dancing, tempting disaster. I honor my responsibility to you, to Connacht. I honor the work you must do. Stay put and attend to that. There are laws in place." Roland continued to stare, his fist still clenched.

"The law; so, if you were killed, and I taken as a spoil of war, the law states I am now possessed by another slave owner, my very thoughts and actions. But that is not true. My soul would never belong to another. No one owns that, not by force. The law states it, yet I would be bound to fight against such. Honor above the law. Hypocrisy? Heretical?"

"That is absurd. Once again, you try to blur the lines between a sacred marriage contract and slavery. You entered into our marriage of your own free will. The Irish cannot be forced to marry. This is your law and custom."

"If you commit murder and are condemned, so am I. Your children and I are stripped of everything. We suffer your consequence. And you say I haven't a voice in this. I do."

"Again, by your Irish law, the family bears responsibility for the deeds of its members," he reminded her. "You confuse my responsibility with your obligation as a wife. And, I agree, everything is upon me. You and our children would be helpless," Roland said, his eyes hard and dark, bearing down on her. This was not the expression of the impassive warrior.

Helpless? Not with the power of Dahlquin behind us, she thought. That was the point of this. Dahlquin, Connacht, Ireland. He needed to understand this. The Solstice dance was but one part of this unity. How had he shifted the argument? Why was she arguing with him at all? Had she learned nothing in the past year?

"You don't understand," he said.

"Neither do you."

A foul odor permeated the foul temper of the chamber.

"Jesus Lord, what is that?" Roland asked, looking about the lightening space.

"Dragon," Eloise murmured, rushing to the old hound laying in her bed. Eloise feared the hound had soiled herself and her bed. But a quick inspection proved it was flatulence. The gentle creature looked shame-faced as Eloise stroked her head. The mighty wire-haired hound had saved her life at the siege, losing a leg and her partner, Beast. She had aged and lost vigor since. Nearly blind and failing, there was still a sparkle in her eyes. Her tail thumped as Eloise caressed and cooed to her, holding her large head against the growing baby in her. *You must be here to raise our pup.*

"That was a fart of the dead," Roland said, standing over them.

It was mean, but it made her smile.

"Roland!" Val shouted before banging on the door, causing all three hounds to bark. Once Roland's squire, Val was now a knight and a brother in spirit. Eloise's horse-brother.

"Come in," Roland said.

"Holy fuck, what died?" Val said, waving his hand in front of his face as he entered. Fido and Griffin welcomed him. "Blessed Saints, sorrow upon me, Ellie, is it Dragon?" he said, walking to them.

Fast on Val's heels came Robin, Roland's squire, and their nephews, Daniel, eleven, and Henry, ten, surrounding her as well.

"She farted," Roland said.

"Ellie or Dragon?" Val asked, kissing the top of Ellie's head.

"Brother," Eloise said, glaring up at him, his blue eyes so teasing. Then she looked at the shocked faces of Robin and the boys.

"Pleasure upon me you didn't kill each other. Lord Hubert said you two are having quite a row," Val said.

Behind Val, Robin, and the boys, came Eloise's servants,

Maggie and Alice, ready to assist Eloise in dressing. Maggie was pregnant with another of Val's bastards, and still angry he wouldn't marry her. Alice was pregnant, and both she and Robin delightedly believed it was his; they were still smitten with each other. Roland forbade such a mismatched marriage between a nobleman of Robin's heritage and a rescued peasant of unknown parentage. *Your parents would never forgive me*, Roland insisted. Consequences of the pilgrimage to Canterbury. Ordained folly. Eloise and Roland eyed each other. Unfinished business. *You don't own me*, she tried to say with her eyes. His stern expression became impassive, as it must be with his men in attendance.

A Winter Solstice Mass was held in the Great Hall, for the servants and workers didn't have the luxury of time or security to leave the castle to attend mass at the churches beyond. Dahlquin Castle's small chapel couldn't accommodate every resident.

The Great Hall was decorated with pine branches, oak, and holly, as could be found. The fire roared in defiance of the December cold. Winter Solstice started the festive season, leading into Christmas and the New Year, ending on Twelfth Night.

All stood, heads bowed. Eloise waited for the blessing and rejuvenation of this hallowed day.

"Blessings upon you," the priest said. "Blessings upon Dahlquin and all who serve. In you, we have strength, survival, and an opportunity to serve God.

"Winter Solstice, the shortest day of the year, the longest, darkest night. How it challenges men's souls. Today we celebrate our God in his earliest creation, the most sacred covenant between God and man: Winter Solstice.

"Before our Christ, Jesus, was born, God created heaven

and earth. He created a sun and moon. A world in balance and harmony with four seasons and a purpose for each. Our earliest people on this island honored that creation, and we still owe our existence to God's benevolence. Today is the day God chose for us to venerate his worldly and heavenly glories: the Sun, his creation, and source of our growth and living, and the Moon, for without the Moon, there is not a balance in tide and humors. We of Ireland are a people older than the birth of Jesus. We can embrace our love and devotion for both, for God is God, and his son, Jesus, is our redeemer.

"We have many stories and myths, but all can trace back to a God and his creation of the sun, moon, heavens, and our earth, where Jesus walked among mortals in the Holy Land, Outremer. Our land is alive with spirits, all part of God's plan, a heavenly body sacredly existing on our blessed island. As Outremer has Noah, Moses, the prophets, Sampson, and Daniel, Ireland has our heroes and holy folk. It was not the Irish who condemned or crucified our Lord on Earth, but the Romans," the priest intoned.

This. All this Eloise wished to convey to Roland when he forbade her from dancing in God's honor with her mother and the women of Dahlquin. A sacred duty to honor God and the Goddess—though the priest neglected that aspect. For even a male priest might be blind and misled by a church often led by power-mad men.

The Goddess was as important as God. That was balance. Did the Romans kill her like they killed Jesus? Could it be, Eloise wondered, that God and Goddess disagreed and bickered as she and Roland? Is that why the Goddess has again been banished from man's religion? The Virgin Mary is the Goddess reborn. How quickly men, and mayhap God, forget. Was this blasphemy? She buried these thoughts and concentrated on the mass.

"Unlike the Romans and other unredeemed pagans," the priest continued, "this is not a day of debauchery and degradation. This is a holy day of blessing and thankfulness. The dark will end, and the light will return. Our ancestors, unknowing of the true God, did honor the glories of God given to them. The return of God's sun. In a few days, we celebrate the new light of humanity, the birth of Jesus.

"And remember, we are Dahlquin. Family, God, crown. For in protecting family, we serve God, leaving Him free to protect others," he said.

"Blessings upon you all, go forth, so much work for us all this day, and the shortest day of the year to accomplish so much. You are loved. You are in God's and Lord Hubert's hands. Amen."

Winter Solstice mass complete, Eloise, Roland, her parents, her servants, and a large retinue—Sir Val, Robin, Daniel, and Henry—left the Great Hall to see the rare glory of tiny, winter-white clouds falling upon Dahlquin.

After days of rain and sleet, it was a magical delight for Winter Solstice. Eloise immediately thought of a snow ride with Roland, to behold all Dahlquin's glories. Their steeds, Garth and Artoch, plunging through the clean white. But she and Roland were in disharmony. Damn. On this of all days.

After a very simple break of fast, the family and attendants headed to the practice grounds within the castle walls.

Old Muireann, the head cook, rushed up to them.

"My lord," she said, bowing her head to Hubert. "My lord," bowing to Roland.

Both men acknowledged her.

"Lady, Ladies," she said to Eloise and her mother. "A word, I beg. Sorrow upon me to bring such tidings on this festive day."

"Of course, Muireann," Aine said, resting on the crutches. "May you have goodness, Lord Husband." Aine both acknowledged and dismissed her husband in one phrase.

HUBERT, Roland, the men, and boys left to attend the morning practice. The wet weather of the previous days left the grounds too wet for horses; only man-to-man practice would happen.

"Roland, this Solstice is like nothing we have done in Leinster," Val said, as they walked to the drill. "Alice and Maggie are beside themselves to be invited to dance. Did you know Aine and Eloise have white surcoats for them to wear, too? Then the longest night of the year. Roland, we are blessed, lucky bastards."

Daniel and Henry, too, were excited at the prospect of the bonfire, stories, and celebration.

"My Lord," Robin said, "Alice says you forbid our Lady to dance. How can you deny Dahlquin? Everyone is talking about it."

"What? Aunt Ellie isn't to dance at the fire?" Henry asked.

"In South Cross, it is a great honor. *Mathair* wouldn't miss it," Daniel said.

"We will all honor the Solstice and God's promise to return the sun, but your Aunt will not dance," Roland said.

"Roland," Val said, "I beg you to reconsider; your jealousy will be your downfall. People think you don't trust them, that you are not truly one of them."

Roland sighed as they walked. Of course, he was jealous. A

deadly sin, he knew, but his wife was not a token for others to behold.

WHAT GRANDER PLACE TO be than the stables of Dahlquin? Though tending the sick and injured brought a tension not so grand. It was frigid, with all the doors open for ventilation.

"Welcome, Good Solstice upon you, Lady," the stable master, Rori, said in greeting.

"And to you, sir."

"Nova is fine, but I knew you would want to know," he said. "Your Lord Husband tells me your hound, Dragon, was poorly this day, too. Sorrow upon me, you should worry so about two beloved creatures on this of all days."

Rori showed Nova's leg, and Eloise could see it was not serious. She continued to stroke Nova, "You are such a good partner, so good with children," she said, stroking the mare. "Blessings upon you for teaching Henry so much. Hopefully, you will do the same with this one," Eloise said, allowing the mare to press her head against her belly. Eloise rubbed gently around Nova's ears, as most horses enjoyed.

Garth heard her voice and grunted to her.

"I am engaged with your predecessor," she called to him. "She taught me so much; you should be grateful." After a pause, "Mayhap we will all go for a snow ride." Such a rare treat.

Eloise looked about the busy stables, stable hands and grooms shoveling the muck from stalls into overflowing wheelbarrows, for the rain and sleet required extensive logistics to remove manure. With horses not being taken out in the foul weather, it was a burden. The stench was fierce, and her eyes watered when she got too close.

Without a word to Rori, Eloise grabbed a hoof pick. After a greeting and a few scratches, she cleaned Garth's hooves. "I know you are bored and wish to move. I do, too," she said, "I will work hard so we might share what is left of this short day."

He peed in anticipation of them going out. She stood aside so as not to get splashed.

"Good boy, but oh, that is potent."

Picking up his left fore, she started to hum, then sing, as she went about his hooves. First, a song of the Holly and Oak Kings. Next a song of the Snow Giants, from a foreign land also fighting for a hold in Ireland, and how the Light of Goodness and Saint Phaidrig had defeated them once and for all, sending them back to their Ice Kingdom in the north. The boys were singing along, as they knew the words, and the men hummed or whistled as Eloise moved from stall to stall, cleaning the hooves of Artoch, Morgund, Mammoth, and the rest. Hooves complete, she took a brush and started grooming. A cat near the ceiling caught her attention. She had similar coloring to Roland's cat, black and orange with hints of white and gray, a roan cat.

"She's a feisty one," Rori said. "So are her kittens, the roan ones."

"Females?" Eloise asked.

"So it seems. These cats sing and dance for the ones they like. Usually, one or two people at most." Rori held up his hand, five gnarled fingers from a lifetime of hard work, nails black from horse dirt. "I still have all my fingers; she likes me."

"I'll take your warning," Eloise said, matching his grin. "She has my respect to keep her distance."

"Lady, if you are going to ride, best start thinking about it,"

Rori advised. "Blessing upon you for your company and song on this cold day, but you will have plenty of work before the bonfire."

"May you have goodness, sir, they all need to get out. I feel such guilt taking only Garth when all eyes look at me with longing." It was not a horse's true life to live stabled, incarcerated, separated from the sky, earth, and herd mates. She walked back to Garth. He greeted her, and she stepped into his damp stall, stroking and scratching. *Do I own you? I would not let another take you, nor sell you. But do I truly own you, your stallion spirit? We work together as partners, but I decide most things. And you comply, most of the time. Goodness upon you,* she chuckled, remembering all the times Garth did not comply, and she had to rethink and redo. *We are bonded since your birth. Before. How would you describe our relationship? You are my legs and together we fly. You possess me, horses possess me in ways I would not change.* She had told Roland he didn't own her. No more than she owned him. They both had—

"Lady Eloise? Is our Lady here?"

Maggie was directed to Garth's stall.

"You need me, Maggie?" she asked, giving Garth what she knew would be their last snuggles for the day, all dreams of a snow ride dashed.

Maggie continued glancing about the stable and the rough-clothed men. She was still uncomfortable in this sanctuary. Maggie's eyes fixed on Eloise as she curtsied, forcing Eloise to look down at her own cloak and garments. How had she gotten this dirty? Good, honest, horse dirt. They owed their survival to horses.

"It is not an emergency, Lady, but your Lady Mother does ask if you might be able to come to the practice field."

"Who is hurt?" Eloise asked, her focus changing.

"Nothing severe. Not an emergency. She begged me to express that. That is why she didn't send Alice or another," Maggie added, showing she could be trusted to deliver a proper message. "But she could use some help. Then you must both prepare for the banquet."

"We will turn out the horses, Lady, worry not," Rori said as they left. Of course, he would, Eloise knew. But it wasn't the same.

THE SNOW WAS STILL COMING DOWN LIGHTLY as Eloise and Maggie reached the practice grounds. Winter Solstice had created a festive, celebratory atmosphere and far more workers and servants had gathered to watch the young boys and youths train with the men. It was like a tournament.

Alice ran to her, putting a hot cup in her hands.

"With your Lady Mother's blessing," Alice said. "She is coming now."

And so she was, crutches and all, one of her attendants carrying two cups.

Eloise took the hot cup, letting the heat warm her hands as she lifted it to her nose, inhaling: mulled wine. She waited for her mother before drinking.

"All is well; the physician is to hand. We should watch," her mother said, holding up her cup, encouraging Eloise to do the same.

"*Mathair*, how is your ankle? Shouldn't you be resting?"

"Rest will come to me, now that you are here," Aine answered, her green eyes sparkling, her nose red with the cold.

There were many pages and squires drilling and practicing

with wooden or real swords. Some engaged in hand-to-hand practice.

Eloise searched the faces. So many to worry about. They were all family. Her father was at the quintain—a post with an arm and flat target surface that spun when struck, requiring the person training to dodge out of the way or strike back—coaching the squires, who were mud-clad, revealing their time on the ground.

"Robin!" Alice cheered as Roland's squire successfully pounded the quintain and escaped the return blow.

Roland was instructing his nephews and two other young pages with their wooden swords. All four boys were muddy and, Eloise thought, mayhap shivering with the cold. Roland watched and counseled as the boys mock fought.

Then Roland drilled with the squires. First Robin, then Lionel, then Robin again. No shields, swords only, one- and two-handed drills. Robin and Lionel were fairly matched as they moved forward and back together, until one of them landed in the mud, too soon for Roland's liking.

The fallen snow upon Roland's chain maille glittered like scales upon a mighty dragon, shining with power, impervious to the winter cold. She was married to that: a winter dragon, her Dragon Lord.

He looked up, scanning the crowd. Finding her.

Such glory and majesty. Behind them, a year of hard-fought successes and losses. Ahead of them, a new year full of promise and a baby, come April.

Every part of her responded. Her hair, her mouth, her teeth. Her toes tingled, and everything up her legs and between. She belonged to him. Despite her declaration.

He smirked as if reading her mind. *Arrogant bastard.* She smirked back and shuddered as gooseflesh raced upon her skin.

"My Lord," Robin asked, "can you show us how it's done?"

"And get myself muddy and miserable as you?" Roland asked.

"Well, I will have to clean your gear," Robin answered.

"Ha," Roland snorted, "you have spoken well. But let me walk you through it one more time," he said. "Why should I tumble in the mud because you have not learned your dance steps?"

Roland drew his sword, *El Muerte Rojo*, which caused another shiver in Eloise, though she had seen it done on more occasions than she could count.

"You know the drill. Rally your force. Find your core. If it helps, feed off the energy of this crowd," he said, pointing to the audience. "Use it. Don't let it be a distraction. Trust yourself."

He waited while both squires looked about the assembly, cold, snow-covered, and raucous.

"No drill. I want you both to go at each other, strike, strike, strike. Dominate that mud and put the other to rest."

This was the awkward part of practice. Holding back, not killing each other. Her father always warned about that detriment. You perfect what you practice. If you practice holding back, what happens on the battlefield? Roland assured her, in a life-or-death situation, most know to unleash. *You did*, he reminded her.

"At-March," Hubert said loudly, striding up, equally devoid of mud and frosted with snow. "A suggestion, Lord."

Eloise could see the challenging smile. What mayhem did her father seek? Already so many struggles on what should have been a festive day of celebration and gratitude.

"The boys need guidance, practice. A demonstration is in order—a father-son dance. Surely, we are too clean."

"Da," Eloise murmured, shaking her head. She did not wish to see her father and husband fight. A terrible idea on any day. She grabbed her mother's hand and they both stared.

Roland turned to face Hubert; had she ever seen such a beaming smile? His one brown tooth, earned from a punch, was highlighted by the white of the rest. The glint in his brown eyes gave her chills on top of the freezing weather. Sword already drawn, he thrust both arms out in welcome.

"It's about damn time you invited me," Roland said with but a hint of the croak, his arms outstretched, hands beckoning. "By your will."

They agreed, and both men went to put on their helms.

ROBIN RAN to get Roland's helm, his cap and chain maille hood already in place. Roland's young nephews, Daniel and Henry, were also in attendance. Val joined Roland's attendants.

"Pay attention. This may be the best lesson of your lives," Roland said to his men and boys. "Watch and learn."

"I pray he doesn't sweep the stables with you," Val said.

"He may," Roland said, looking from Val to Robin and his nephews. "That is the price I pay for education—yours and mine. I may not remember what happens and will need you to tell me," Roland said to the wide-eyed youths. He was grinning, though he wasn't sure they could see it with his helm in place. "Remember this: face your fear, your doubt." He didn't say *your defeat*. No, he would not voice that; he was here to teach and learn. "Bleeding saints, step into it and be willing to learn. It is a great honor when a master asks you to spar."

"Blessings upon you, Lord, and luck," Robin said.

"Luck upon you, Uncle," both nephews said.

"Fuck," Val said.

Roland ignored his friend's worry as he turned to meet Hubert.

Roland and Hubert circled each other as the snow continued to drift down. As with the other combatants, no shields, swords only, and no one was supposed to die, yet accidents happened. Often.

Hubert made the first strike, and Roland met it and repelled it. Again, Hubert struck. Roland defended. Swords meeting, clanging, crashing. Roland took an opportunity to try for Hubert's chest, not a deadly blow, but a hard tag, so all knew the vulnerability. Hubert deflected, but Roland was able to move his sword tip to Hubert's throat, at the same instant Roland felt Hubert's sword tip at his throat. *Damn*. A draw.

Both nodded agreement and, withdrawing swords, stepped back to renew the training.

Roland considered that mayhap Hubert, at fifty years old, would fatigue before he did and hoped to tease and dodge if this were true. But this was the Barbarian, Lord Hubert of Dahlquin.

Again, Hubert took the offense, thrusting for the throat. Roland deflected, Hubert spun and came back at his sword arm. Roland twisted in time to meet the sword; the guards on the swords locked as both men heaved against each other.

Thinking to use Hubert's momentum, Roland yielded, allowing Hubert to fall into him, striking his exposed neck as he fell forward. No neck, no Hubert. The other man used the same strategy.

They circled again. Attack. The guards of their swords locked once more, and Roland reacted again by giving in to Hubert's strength, using the momentum against him. This time, Hubert fell forward, and Roland heaved his sword around to hit Hubert in the ribs. But Hubert righted himself enough as he stumbled, meeting Roland's sword with a full blow and sending Roland off balance. *Be faster*, Roland thought, bracing himself as Hubert returned, thrusting for the throat once more. As Hubert's sword tip reached the throat, Roland hit Hubert in the ribs with the flat side of his blade. Enough to show how vulnerable Hubert was, without inflicting true damage. Both men were awarded a strike and the circling began anew.

"Roland!" Hubert shouted, "We are dancing like a pair of maidens afraid of soiling our garments."

"I wanted you to look good tonight," Roland answered, sounding like a growl from his damaged voice and heavy breathing. Hell, his throat hurt from all the tags he'd received. *Focus*. He studied Hubert for a hint of his next attack.

Hubert led with his right shoulder, sword low, coming in for a hard strike. Roland braced and blocked, but lost his footing in the mud as his left foot slipped forward. *No*, but he was going down. Swinging his sword, he hit Hubert's thigh with a satisfying thud as his arse, then back, then back of his head hit the mud, the freezing ooze seeping into his garments. "Fuck," he muttered, his own sword up defensively anticipating Hubert. But Hubert had his sword firmly in Roland's belly. Roland exhaled as more cold mud seeped into his garments.

"Virginity lost. Get up. We're not done!" Hubert barked.

Roland could hear the roars of laughter and cheers as he rolled over and got up. He saluted Hubert, then gave a bow. Next, he turned to his men and boys and saluted them. Arms outstretched, he waved to the noisy, boisterous crowd, then gave them a deep bow, as well. Aine and Eloise were still clutching each other, worry or cold, he didn't know. He kissed his muddy palm and threw the kiss in Eloise's direction. A bit late, she did reach to catch it and put her small, gloved hands to her lips.

Keep moving, or you will freeze, he told himself, facing Hubert once more. He circled, watching. Hubert pivoted. Differently. He was injured or faked. Roland kept circling, striking, searching for Hubert's injury. His leg. Maybe. The crafty bastard might be trying to lure him in. *Learning upon me*, Roland thought as he rushed in, first feigning to strike right, engaging Hubert's sword and twisting hard up and 'round left. Roland pushed hard, knowing if Hubert toppled, he would go down, too.

Hubert was down, and Roland pushed himself off, quickly pinning him to the ground with the tip of his sword at Hubert's throat, only to feel Hubert's sword as firmly between his legs. Roland inhaled. Exhaled.

Draw, again.

Roland extended a hand and pulled Hubert up from the muddy goo.

"Do you wish to concede?" Hubert asked.

"This is your dance, Lord, your call. Surely, I have more to learn."

"Much," Hubert said, with a slight grin.

Those still braving the cold and snow cheered for more.

Hubert and Roland looked at their women. Aine and Eloise both looked stricken, and both were shaking their heads.

"I think they do not wish for you to concede, Lord," Hubert said.

"Agreed," Roland said.

Hubert shoved Roland back from him, keeping to the less slick ground.

Roland shoved him back, and Hubert slipped, but recovered before Roland could take advantage. Swords up, they charged in over and over, turning, swinging, locking guards, pushing away, and striking again. Now, it was a dance, with a cadence, balance, the building energy, and the music of metal to metal. Roland tasted blood. Cut lip?

Surely, his neck bled from the tags of Hubert's sword tip.

Hubert came in hard and fast, a two-handed grip on his sword. Roland dodged, then slipped, and Hubert's swing turned to an unintended bludgeon upon Roland's head.

Through the crushing sound of Hubert's gauntlet and pommel upon his helm, full metal contact, Roland swore he heard breaking bones. His skull?

He turned, gasping, his left eye the source of the blood and flashing stars. He wasn't sure what he was seeing, blood amidst the falling snow.

"Enough! Your dance is over."

Who said that? Was it over? But he knew Hubert was upon him. Lifting his sword, he swung hard, hitting wood. A crutch. *Bleeding, fucking saints on a cross, he had killed his mother-in-law. Jesus Lord.*

A kick to the groin. He buckled at the knees, dropped to his elbows, and there was the crutch. He couldn't hold his head up and put his forehead upon the muddy wood.

There was noise, voices. He was breathing but couldn't move.

"Roland!" Eloise called.

"Don't touch him. Let him be," Val said.

"He's hurt."

"Touching him will only make it worse, trust me. A man gets over such agony in his own time."

"He could be dying!"

"He thinks he is, but he won't."

Roland managed to hold up a fist in agreement with Val.

"You saw that crutch, didn't you? How it bounced off the ground?" Val said, with a grin Eloise didn't understand. "God's eyes, I wouldn't have believed such a thing if I hadn't seen it. Hit poor Roland where it hurts most. Your mother threw the death blow." Val, Robin, and the nephews started laughing.

"It's a damn long short day for Roland," Val said to more laughter.

Roland took a few more breaths and thought he could push himself to his knees.

"Can you take your helm off?" Eloise asked.

"Aine!" Hubert shouted. "Have you lost your mind?"

"Have you?" she snapped back at him.

"Of course. Fighting like that. You know better than to try and break up a dog fight," Hubert said. "And it wasn't your call."

"I know the sound of breaking bones. Since you two lumbering behemoths wouldn't listen to my words, I threw the crutch at Roland. He was the closest."

"And you may well have killed your son-in-law. Look at the poor sot."

"You've broken your shield hand. Spit that blood out before you choke," she commanded. "Go clean up, both of you; we have a banquet to attend and a Solstice ceremony, which neither of you are to dance at. Go!" she said, pointing to the residential tower. The physician was running behind them.

They trudged to the Great Hall, and many rushed to tend to their Lord. Did he need drink? Some food? How were his injuries? And Lord At-March, such an amazing battle, two lords, like two kings, light and dark. After accepting the accolades, Roland and Hubert continued to the residential tower. Roland was glad for the silence between them; he had much roiling in his mind and heart.

Hubert and Roland exited the physician's chamber and limped back to their chambers to clean and dress.

"Do you think you have learned not to cross Lady Dahlquin?" Hubert asked, in a mumbling voice.

"Did you?" Roland asked with a wry grin.

"I learned that a long time ago," Hubert said, "And I never provoked her to take up arms against me, as you did."

Roland gave a small snort.

The two men kept moving as Roland pondered Hubert's comments and remembered Aine's. He had never heard her speak out against her husband as she did today.

"You have shown courage and fortitude. But you still have much to learn about Dahlquin. Connacht," Hubert said.

Roland felt himself stiffen, checking his posture—straight spine, shoulders back, ready for action.

Hubert didn't react, but kept his limping pace.

"I try. I try very hard to stay out of your marriage. Your bedchamber," Hubert said in a stern tone. "You and Eloise must find your way together. However, you must provide more—" He paused searching for words.

They kept moving, not looking at each other.

"They—my Lady wife and daughter—were born to serve a higher power. I have come to accept this. Aine was born to serve Connacht before she was my wife. Her power, her grace." He paused, as if seeking more words. "She is what I can never be. Dahlquin is stronger for it."

"She serves you well," Roland said.

"She serves Dahlquin well, and in ways I do not understand. But I trust."

Eloise and Roland walked into her mother's chamber to retrieve the Solstice garments, still laid carefully across the wedding chest.

The doors between her parents and Eloise's own adjoining chambers were all open, as the couples dressed for the Winter Solstice bonfire.

Aine's servant, Daire, had her mother's garments across her arm, ready to assist the Lady dressing. Eloise lifted hers, placing it over her arm as well, gazing at the chest, the flat top, so inviting to sit upon. She bent over and placed her hand upon the familiar oak, solid, protective, ceremonial.

"A well-made piece," Roland said.

"It is," she agreed. "A wedding gift from my grandfather to my mother, welcoming her to Dahlquin." She turned to him, explaining the symbolism, Irish and English, the lovely, feminine flowers, and the heart.

"England, but I thought your grandfather came from Wales? Shouldn't it have been a Welsh dragon?" he asked.

Dragons, she thought with a sigh, smiling up at Roland.

"You are correct, though it is—was—tribute to King Henry the Second. Surely you would agree to that honor?" she said.

He nodded, glancing again at the chest.

"Away with you; I've our Lady to dress," Daire said, shooing them out of the chamber.

"Take our excuse, fair Daire," Roland said, putting his hand at Eloise's lower back, guiding her out.

Eloise insisted on wearing the ceremonial Solstice surcoat over the bleached woolen chemise. No harm in that, Roland agreed. The garments were not the problem. Neither he nor Eloise mentioned dancing. In the borrowed white Solstice surcoat, Maggie plaited Eloise's hair. Alice, also in white, looked on in reverence and awe. It seemed not a man in Dahlquin had a qualm about his woman dancing for this Solstice ceremony; at least Roland heard no dissent. *The difference between jealousy and security*, he thought.

Doors still open, all could hear Hubert and Aine, their voices getting louder as they approached Roland's and Eloise's chamber.

"All will be as it should. I will be dancing for three," Aine said in her confident, melodious voice.

"You're a cripple," Hubert said, mumbling, the side of his mouth abraded inside and out, Roland suspected.

"Not in spirit. Besides, Eloise wasn't here last year. We survived."

"She lost the baby."

"She did. She was too sick to dance. There is a difference."

Hubert said nothing.

"Speaking of crippled, a broken hand, your leg limping, and your mouth," she was saying as they entered the chamber. "And look at his eye," she said to Hubert, pointing to Roland as they entered the chamber. "You could have been blinded," she said to Roland.

Roland stood and bowed as Lord Hubert and Lady Aine entered.

The men looked at each other and grinned, lopsided and cracked, each suppressing a chuckle.

"The leeches helped," Eloise said. "His eye is open now."

"Gratitude upon me, Lord, I learned much this day, blessings upon you," Roland said.

Hubert nodded.

The Solstice garments were stunning, reflecting the sconce and candlelight in the chamber, shimmering hope and brilliance. Mother and daughter embraced, hugging as if they had been estranged for long months, rather than minutes. Their tears also reflected the life-giving light: a joyous mother, daughter, and unborn.

The sun and moon and stars, the light of life; he was married to that.

Hubert was at his side, speechless as Roland. Speechless in their humility.

A servant, followed by Val, Robin, Daniel, and Henry was at the door to announce the fire was lit.

"Oh, Auntie, Great Auntie," Henry said, looking back and forth from Eloise to Aine. "You are so beautiful."

"But won't you be cold?" Daniel asked.

"Blessings upon you both," Eloise said, putting her arms out for the boys.

They ran to her and Aine for hugs.

The women were bundled in coats of fur against the snow. Aine was on crutches. *Fuck, these women are relentless,* Roland thought as they all left.

ROLAND HELD Eloise's hand as they walked to the great bonfire. Hubert carried Aine, despite his injuries. Hubert's squire carried the crutches, while the rest of the entourage followed. Through the snowy darkness of the long night, Roland could see torches lighting the way for many of Dahlquin's farmers, workers, families, and children, bringing stools and planks to sit upon, all in dark oil cloaks, faces barely visible in the dim light. The falling snow reflected the firelight. Eloise squeezed his hand as she looked up to him.

"It is a glory," he said, taking in the whole sight before them.

They chuckled as they overheard some others grumbling: "Couldn't we do this in the Great Hall?"

The Dahlquins and At-Marchs found their benches covered in snow. The men gallantly brushed the snow off with their arms, and eagerly took the giggling women in their laps. Daniel and Henry fit quietly in between. Only the musicians had the benefit of an oil cloth canopy to protect their instruments.

Hubert stood, addressing his people: "All know why we are here, as in the Beginning, there was darkness and light. Our ancestors, far and wide, wondered and quaked in the looming darkness. Each year, the sun returned in early or late season with God's whim. It is not ours to know, but to honor and prepare. Though the word of God and God's son took some time to reach us here, God had not forsaken his people. We honor the world He created; the beasts, plants, rivers, understanding the heavenly touch upon us. There are many stories and legends of this mighty Solstice season. We have recited many all month, most especially today and this very night.

"This cold, snowy night beckons faith and rejuvenation, but also dictates, with prudence, to jump straight to the Solstice fire dance."

"Seems we had a mighty battle between dark and light this day—and light prevailed," someone said, to cheers and chuckles, referring to Hubert and Roland.

"The light of our Lady Aine," said another, bringing more laughter and murmurs.

Eloise took Roland's hand and placed it on her lips, kissing his gloved palm before placing it on her belly. "You are my light," she murmured. "I love you."

"The highlight, the greatest honor, is upon us," Hubert said.

"Dahlquin honors the ancestors and our God, as our ladies rise up, despite the darkness and snow, and give our blessings and gratitude for renewal."

Aine stood, and all her attendants came to help her. All black figures in cloaks.

Roland held Eloise close, and she nestled into his embrace. *One with me.* Her kiss and words were fresh in his mind. He took her gloved hand and kissed it. "By your will, you are the glory of Connacht." He pushed her from his lap. "Help your mother." *I may not understand, but your father trusts, and I will too.*

He watched his wife, teary eyed, run to assist her mother to her place, then run to the other end of the fire pit—just as a dark wave of figures, the women of Dahlquin, came forth.

ONCE AINE WAS STANDING, crutches securely in place, surrounded by her ladies and cousins, Eloise ran to the opposite end of the fire pit, Maggie and Alice on either side of her. The rest of the women filled in around the circle. All familiar faces, with long histories in Dahlquin.

The musicians started a slow winter ballad, and the dance began. The women joined hands, raising and dropping them as they sang praises to the land, the sky, the trees, and the rivers. They sang of God's glory and the bounty provided. Ancient songs, the words adapted to the Christian faith. The song changed, the tempo picked up, and the women, still holding hands, started a line dance. Adapting to her disability, Aine swayed in place, and as each woman passed her, they clutched hands, kissed, and continued the dance. There was stumbling, as some fell behind, smiles and laughter as the dance proceeded. The tempo picked up, so did the warmth, and on cue, the women shed their dark cloaks, wrapping the cloaks tightly into balls to keep the inside dry, before setting them down in the cold snow.

The assembly gasped and clapped for all the women clad in white, even the attendants, who created the dazzling, intoxicating, and reverent atmosphere. The farmers and servants wore their woolen chemises on the outside to provide the lightest color. Eloise knew she and her mother were resplendent in their ceremonial Solstice surcoats. Such honor and responsibility upon them.

A rousing song of joy and renewed fertility played, and the women danced in a freestyle form, swaying or gyrating with the music, exalting in life, in this moment of warmth by the fire. *We look like snow fairies flirting with fire, and this requires a song,* Eloise thought, committing the image to memory, as she danced upon the frozen ground and saw the frigid sky above her. The grand contrasts of this night, light and dark, fire and ice. She bent down, her hands finding the ground, slowly coming up her legs, grasping her belly, feeling her veins and tissue, a protective shield for her baby. Her hands continued up to her breasts, so tender and pain-filled in the early weeks of pregnancy, once again fresh and aware of sensual delights. She thrust her hands to the dark, overcast sky, the heavens. Sacred power filled her, and she felt such gratitude to partake and give back, with a child, a son of Dahlquin. God and Goddess—she may not be spoken of in this Christian world, but Eloise, and surely these other women, felt Her in this moment, and every moment. You are not forgotten, Goddess. Somewhere off in the distance, even above the music, Eloise heard the wolves, their song, the validation. We are not forgotten.

The snow had continued to fall while Eloise was caught up in the moment. The fire was going out. *This is not how the cere-*

mony was to go, Eloise thought. *The fire gives hope. If it goes out, such bad tidings.* Again, the image of snow fairies came to her, spirits of all nature, consumed in a dance of survival, life. But light is life, and the snow fairies were overwhelming it.

The assembly felt it too. This was terrible. Would winter last forever in Connacht? None wanted perpetual winter with no crops, no new livestock. The tales of great, unrelenting mounds of snow upon the land. The dreaded winter giants. If and when summer ever returned, it would be a great flood of melting snow and mud sucking them all in.

Eloise could hear the rising murmurs among one or two, but knew the tide of fear might take hold. *How could they be so easily dismayed? When moments before, all were as enraptured with the beauty before them as she had been? How could they have so little faith?*

Aine knelt, crawled into the fire pit and blew on an ember. It sparked. She cupped her hand around the tiny flame, allowing it to grow for those closest to witness. Eloise fell to her knees to do the same, "Help her," she called to the dancers. They were all on their hands and knees, reviving the fire with their breath.

They were fighting a losing battle against the increasing snowfall. Aine sat back as best she could and held her hands out, encouraging her dancers to do the same.

"Winter is upon us, the snow is proof of that and cannot be turned," Aine said, looking about the assembly. "And you see," Aine said, "together, we will survive. Together, we are strong. United in purpose. Loyal. Fear not the winter." Aine stood as the snow extinguished the embers.

"Let the longest night commence, and may it be filled with hope and glory in our God and ancestors. Dahlquin will prevail."

Sighs, clapping, cheering, murmurs, and grumbling children with cold, freezing, wet feet began their treks to beds.

As Eloise retrieved her fur cloak, Roland was there, his arms out, coat and cloak open to her, then, like dragon's wings wrapping around her, warm and protective.

COLD AND TIRED, the family entourage made its way to the residential chambers, where Hubert and Aine bid a sweet and hasty Solstice farewell.

The torchlight of the hallway was reduced by one.

The hounds shook, ridding themselves of melted snow.

Roland gazed at his group: Val, Robin, Maggie, Alice, and his nephews.

"Boys, you would do us great service if you got yourselves to bed promptly and unaided," he said to Daniel and Henry. "I know you are cold and wet, but this night, do for yourselves."

"We can, Uncle," both agreed, nodding. Henry yawned, causing most everyone else to yawn.

"You are not to wander the castle; the guards may take you for Solstice sprites and throw you off the ramparts. Keep to your beds."

They nodded solemnly again.

"I believe my Lady and I are capable of disrobing ourselves," he said, looking at Eloise. Her smile of delight revealed her agreement. "With my leave, take to your own beds. We shall meet again on the morrow," he said to the rest.

"May you have goodness, Lord," Robin said, "and a hearty Solstice to you."

"Blessings upon you, Roland, Sister," Val said with a smile and bow.

Gloomy Maggie seemed as giddy as Alice at the prospect of getting the evening off.

"Hearty Solstice to you all, as well," Roland said, wrapping his arm around Eloise, guiding her towards their bedchamber, torch held out in the other.

"Lady, I will be retrieving your Solstice garments on the morrow and return them to your mother's chamber," Maggie called back to them.

"Goodness upon you, Maggie," Eloise said.

Opening their chamber door, Roland asked, "Do you desire such a chest? As your mother has?"

"The wedding chest?" she asked, entering the chamber.

"Of course, it wouldn't be from my father. But—" He closed the door after the hounds were in, heading to light the sconces and candles while Eloise checked the warming pots.

So much to attend to without servants, he remembered.

"Goodness upon you, Roland, that is such a kindness. Mayhap, we can speak of it another time." Though she wore her gloves, she fondled her ring finger. "Tonight, I am grateful to have you, your mother's ring, and our growing son," she said, wrapping her arms about her belly. "Tonight, this is enough."

UNDRESSING, Eloise marveled again how Roland appeared as a Dragon Lord, strong, unrelenting, impervious to cold. Without the chain maille, his dark locks hung above his shoulders; the dark hairs on his chest were his new scales, protecting and insulating. His swollen left eye was barely open. The bruising would be terrible.

"Tonight, at the bonfire, you and your mother looked like dragons breathing fire," Roland said.

"Winter Dragons," she said with a sigh, telling him of her images of him.

He snorted, a wry smile forming.

"Get into bed, woman, it has been a long damn day, and I need to enjoy the longest night of the year."

"This is what we have been waiting for," she said, climbing in.

Once under the blankets, they embraced, and she felt his hot mouth on hers. The image of him as a dragon was so vivid, his leg seemed like a mighty tail, and it cracked as it wrapped around hers, pulling her legs apart to cold winter air, shocking and arousing at once, as he moved over her. His kisses were fire as their tongues danced, reigniting to flame again and again. "If I offer my manhood, you won't burn it, will you?" he asked jokingly, already rotating and assuming the position.

"Or me," she mumbled. A dragon phallus was a new delicacy.

But burn, he did. She gasped and squealed as his dragon's tongue teased her. He took her inner thigh in his teeth, then he lifted, arching over her belly, placing himself on her chest, between her breasts. She quivered in the power of his taut muscles, body hair as scales, instead of the wolf pelt she often envisioned.

"We need a drink," he mumbled.

"We—what?" Eloise asked, feeling the cold air up the length of her as he got up to get a cup. All she needed was him.

"To stall, eh? I'll be done if I don't take some rest. Don't we wish to make this a long night?"

She listened to him move about the familiar chamber in the

dark, carefully shuffling, lest one of the hounds be awakened. But they heard him and were at his side, tails thumping to be of service. Patting and murmuring to the hounds, "Good dog, Dragon," he said, "by your will, do not die this night." He found the pitcher of wine on the table, poured a cup, and returned to bed, feeling his way, one hand outstretched to her with the cup of wine. Still aroused, her clenched fingers could barely hold the cup.

"Hurry up; I'll spill it," she said, as she felt him climb into bed.

"You won't," he said firmly, taking the cup from her. "*Sláinte*. To your health and the baby's," he said, touching the cup to her belly.

"And to yours, Roland."

She had one sip; he slowly drained the cup as they sat together on this long night, the blankets pulled up around their shoulders. Roland took her hand, held her palm to his lips and kissed it.

"Dulcinea, there is so much I would tell you. So much I try to show you. I need you safe. And content," he said, in a soft, scratchy voice. "I will search for words another day, eh? Tonight, l will show you. Let us share our dance this long night, as we hoped."

"Let us start again," she said, lying back down. "My toes are cold," she said, as the bed had cooled off substantially.

He lay down and pulled her onto him.

"Indeed, you have lost your vigor," she said, as she ground against his less robust self.

"Mayhap if you blow on me, as you did the fire."

It wasn't necessary. Once again, she felt him grow between her legs as if by magic, a limp piece of flesh becoming a thing of splendor. *Was everyone in Dahlquin enjoying such a night?* His hands caressed her breasts, igniting another blaze. She tried to mount him, and he took her hips in his hands, slowing her down.

They kissed and fondled, warming the bedding.

"I must," she said, resisting him. "We may do it again. And again. The night is long."

He held her hips tightly, before lifting and shifting her to the side.

"As dragons," he said, rolling her over on her stomach, "unless that is painful to the baby."

"It is not, if you don't lay your full weight upon us."

"Everything but my full weight," he rasped, as he entered her, "and don't unfurl your wings."

She wanted to laugh at the thought of a dragon's wings opening and poking him in his good eye. How did dragons manage such a thing as mating?

"Do you think they mate in flight?" she asked, and gasped as he moved his hands from the bed to her shoulders.

"I'm—flying—now," he whispered, rhythmically.

She didn't answer, but knew the power of the dragon within her, each thrust pounded like beating wings as the winter dragon took flight. She matched him, feeling the strength, seeing snow, silver bright, against the black night. His heat and the winter's ice. How could this be? It was dark, but they were aglow, the way lit. Her gasps turned to a flaming moan as he took her neck in his mouth. Hands clenched, toes curled, she shuddered in release, cascading, giving all to the dragon while demanding more.

Sweating and joyous, Eloise rolled on her back and nestled into Roland's arms. Though near asleep, he put his large hand on her protruding belly, a dragon's massive claws protecting their egg. She fell asleep, secure and one with her Dragon Lord.

Anne M. Beggs is writing an adventure romance saga, starting in 1224 AD, Connacht, Ireland. She is driven to capture and write about unheard voices of the past, voices that speak to injustice and hazard, and a spiritual quest for understanding and meaning. For Eloise of Dahlquin, in *Archer's Grace, Book One of the Dahlquin Series*, she must discover her inner hero and not wait to be saved. Then, she must help others be their own heroes: stronger together. Eloise returns in "The Dragon Lord" in *Unlocked*, continuing her spiritual quest for understanding. Please follow Anne M. Beggs on Facebook, Bookbub, and Instagram, and visit her website at annembeggs.com.

About Paper Lantern Writers

The Paper Lantern Writers are an author collective focused on historical fiction of all eras. From Medieval Europe to Gilded Age America (and beyond), our books will take you on the journeys of a lifetime.

Find us at www.paperlanternwriters.com

facebook.com/paperlanternwriters

twitter.com/writers_paper

instagram.com/paperlanternwriters

AUTHORS' NOTE

The model for our "old wooden chest" is a 15th Century French piece, purchased in 1957 by the Metropolitan Museum of Art, currently housed in the Cloisters Collection. The chest features two carved coats of arms: one representing France and the other the Dauphin, as well as the oft-referenced heart-shaped lock.

Made in the USA
Middletown, DE
04 November 2022

13851303R00126